His lips touched hers, settling over their softness.

'Why are you doing this?' The words spilled out.

'Because it feels right,' Cole murmured.

'But I'm not really a...a date, am I?' Liz argued. 'Cole, please...' anguished uncertainty in her eyes '...we have to work together.'

'We do work together. We work very well together.' He stroked the worry line between her brows. 'I'm just taking it to another level...'

Initially a French/English teacher, **Emma Darcy** changed careers to computer programming before marriage, motherhood, and the happy demands of keeping up with three lively sons and the very social life of her businessman husband, Frank. Very much a people person, and always interested in relationships, she finds the world of romance fiction a thrilling one.

Emma Darcy is the award-winning Australian author of more than 80 Modern Romance® novels. Her compelling, sexy, intensely emotional novels have gripped the imagination of readers around the globe. She's sold nearly 60 million books worldwide and won enthusiastic praise:

"Emma Darcy delivers a spicy love story…
a fiery conflict and a hot sensuality"
—*Romantic Times*

Recent titles by the same author:

THE BEDROOM SURRENDER
THE BILLIONAIRE BRIDEGROOM
THE BLIND-DATE BRIDE

HIS BOARDROOM MISTRESS

BY
EMMA DARCY

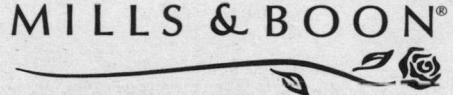

Many thanks to Phil Asker and his wonderful team for providing me
with so many amazing experiences on The Captain's Choice Tour of
South-East Asia—all in such a safe and friendly atmosphere. Great memories!

*First published in Great Britain 2003
Harlequin Mills & Boon Limited,
Eton House, 18-24 Paradise Road, Richmond, Surrey TW9 1SR*

© Emma Darcy 2003

ISBN 0 263 83703 3

*Set in Times Roman 10½ on 12½ pt.
01-0104-42125*

*Printed and bound in Spain
by Litografía Rosés, S.A., Barcelona*

CHAPTER ONE

'THE kind of man you want, Liz, is the marrying kind.'

The quiet authority of her mother's voice cut through the buzz of suggestions being tossed around by her three sisters, all of whom had succeeded in marrying the men of their choice. This achievement made them feel qualified to hand out advice which Liz should take, now that she had been forced to confess her failure to get a commitment from the man who'd been her choice.

Brendan had told her he felt their relationship was stifling him. He needed space. So much space he was now in Nepal, half a world away from Sydney, planning to find himself or lose himself in the Himalayas, meditate in a Buddhist monastery, anything but make a life with a too managing woman.

It was shaming, humiliating to have to admit his defection to her family, but there was no excuse for not attending her father's sixtieth birthday luncheon today and no avoiding having to explain Brendan's absence.

The five of them—her mother, her sisters and herself—were in the kitchen, cleaning up after the long barbecue lunch which had been cooked by the male members of the family, now relaxing out on the patio of her parents' home, minding the children playing in the backyard.

Liz knew she had to face up to her situation and try to move on from it, but right now she felt engulfed by a sense of emptiness—three years of togetherness all drained away—and her mother's statement hit a very raw place.

'How can you know if they're the marrying kind or not?' she tossed back derisively.

Mistake!

Naturally, her wonderfully successful siblings had the answers and leapt in to hit Liz over the head with them.

'First, you look for a man with a good steady job,' her oldest sister, Jayne, declared, pausing in her task of storing leftovers in the refrigerator to deliver her opinion. 'You want someone to support you when the kids come along.'

Jayne was thirty-four, the mother of two daughters, and married to an accountant who'd never deviated from forging a successful career in accountancy.

'Someone with a functional family background,' Sue contributed with a wise look. 'They value what they've had and want it for themselves.'

Sue was thirty-two, married to a solicitor from a big family, now the besotted father of twin sons, loving his wife all the more for having produced them.

Liz silently and bitterly conceded two black marks against Brendan who'd never held a steady job—preferring to pick up casual work in the tourist industry—and had no personal experience of a functional family background since he'd been brought up by a series of foster parents.

There was no longer any point in arguing that she earned enough money to support them both. A small family, as well, if Brendan would have been content to be a house husband, as quite a few men were these days. The traditional way was not necessarily the *only* way, but Jayne and Sue weren't about to appreciate any other view but theirs, especially with the current inescapable proof that Liz's way hadn't worked.

'What about your boss?'

The speculative remark from her younger sister, Diana, jolted Liz out of maundering over her failures. 'What about him?' she retorted tersely, reminded that Diana, at only twenty-eight, was rather smug at having scooped the marriage pool by snagging her own boss, the owner of a chain of fashion boutiques for which she was still a buyer since they had no immediate plans to start a family.

'Everyone knows Cole Pierson is rolling in money, probably a billionaire by now. Isn't his divorce due to go through? He's been separated from his wife for ages and she's been gallivanting around, always in the social pages, linked to one guy or another. I'd certainly count Cole Pierson available and very eligible,' Diana declared, looking at Liz as though she'd been lax at not figuring that out for herself.

'Get real! That doesn't mean *available* to me,' Liz threw back at her, knowing full well she didn't have the female equipment to attract a man of his top-line attributes.

'Of course it does,' Diana persisted. 'He's only

thirty-six to your thirty, Liz, and right on the spot for you to snaffle. You could get him if you tried. After all, being his P.A. is halfway there. He depends on you…'

'Cole Pierson is not the least bit interested in me as a woman,' Liz snapped, recoiling absolutely from the idea of man-hunting where no love or desire was likely to be kindled.

Besides, she'd long ago killed any thought of her boss *that way* and she didn't want to do anything that might unsettle what had become a comfortable and satisfying business relationship. At least she could depend on *its* continuing into the foreseeable future.

'Why would he be interested?' Diana countered, apparently deciding she'd done her share of the cleaning up, propping herself on a stool at the island bench and examining her fingernails for any chipped varnish. 'You've been stuck with Brendan all the time you've been working for Cole Pierson, not giving out any availability signals,' she ran on.

'He is quite a hunk in the tall, dark and handsome mould,' Jayne chimed in, her interest sparked by the possibility of Liz linking up with the financial wizard who managed the money of several of her accountant husband's very wealthy clients. As she brought emptied salad bowls to the sink where their mother was washing up and Liz drying, she made a more direct remark. 'You must feel attracted to him, Liz.'

'No, I don't,' she swiftly denied, though she certainly had been initially, when he'd still been human and happily married. He'd been very distractingly attractive *then*, but being the remarkable man he was and having a beautiful wife in the background, Liz had listed him in the no hope category.

Besides, she'd just found Brendan—a far more realistic and reachable choice for her—so she'd quelled any wayward feelings towards her boss.

'How couldn't you be?' Sue queried critically, frowning over what she assumed was totally unnatural. 'The few times I've dropped in on you at your office and he's appeared...the guy is not only a stunner but very charming. Fantastic blue eyes.'

Cold blue eyes, Liz corrected.

Cold and detached.

Ever since he'd lost his baby son eighteen months ago—a tragic cot death—Cole had retreated inside himself. The separation from his wife six months later had not come as a surprise to Liz. The marriage had to be in trouble. Her boss had moved beyond *connecting* to anyone.

He switched on a superficial charm for clients and visitors but there was no real warmth in it. He had a brilliant brain that never lost track of the money markets, that leapt on any profitable deal for his clients' investments, that paid meticulous attention to every critical detail of his business. But it was also a brain that blocked any intrusion to whatever he thought and felt on a personal level. Around him was an impenetrable wall, silently but strongly emitting the message—*keep out*.

'There's just no spark between us,' she told Sue, wanting to dampen this futile line of conversation. 'Cole is totally focused on business.'

Which made *him* appreciate her management skills,

she thought with black irony. He certainly didn't feel *stifled* by her being efficient at keeping track of everything. He expected it of her and it always gave her a kick when she surprised him by covering even more than he expected. He was a hard taskmaster.

'You need to shake him out of that one-track mind-set,' Diana advised, persisting with her get-the-boss idea.

'You can't change what drives a person's life,' Liz flashed back at her, realising she'd been foolish to think she could change any of Brendan's ingrained attitudes.

Diana ignored this truism. 'I bet he takes you for granted,' she rattled on, eyeing Liz assessingly. 'Treats you as part of the office furniture because you don't do anything to stand out from it. Look at you! When was the last time you spent money on yourself?'

Liz gritted her teeth at the criticism. It was all very well for Diana, who had a rich husband to pay for everything she wanted. *She* didn't need to siphon off most of her income to make the payments on a city apartment. Liz had figured the only way she'd ever have a home to call her own was to buy it herself. Besides which, real estate was a good solid investment.

'I keep up a classic wardrobe for work,' she argued, not bothering to add she had no use for fancy clothes anyway. She and Brendan had never gone anywhere fancy, preferring a much more casual lifestyle, using whatever spare money they had to travel where they could. Jeans, T-shirts and jackets took them to most places.

'Dullsville,' Diana said witheringly. 'All black suits and sensible shoes. In fact, you've let yourself get positively drab. What you need is a complete makeover.'

Having finished putting everything away, her two older sisters joined Diana on stools around the island bench and jumped on this bandwagon. 'I've never thought long hair suits you,' Jayne remarked critically. 'It swamps your small face. And when you wear it pulled back like that, it does nothing for you at all. Makes your facial bones appear sharper. No softening effect. You really should get it cut and styled, Liz.'

'And coloured,' Sue said, nodding agreement. 'If you must wear black suits, mouse brown hair doesn't exactly give you a lift.'

'There's no *must* about it,' Diana declared, glaring a knowing challenge as she added, 'I bet you simply took the cheap route of having a minimal work wardrobe. Am I right or not, Liz?'

She couldn't deny it. Not making regular visits to a hairdresser saved her time and money and it was easy enough to slick back her long hair into a tidy clip at the back of her neck for work. Besides, Brendan had said he liked long hair. And the all-purpose suits she wore meant she didn't have to think about putting something smarter together—a sensible investment that actually cost less than a more varied range of clothes.

'What does it matter?' she countered with a vexed

sigh at being put under the microscope like this. 'I get by on it,' she added defiantly. 'Nobody criticises me at work.'

'The invisible handmaiden,' Diana scoffed. 'That's what you've let yourself become, and you could be a knockout if you made the effort.'

'Oh, come off it!' she protested, losing patience with the argument. 'I've always been the plain one in this family. And the shortest.'

She glared at tall, willowy Jayne with her gorgeous mane of dark wavy hair framing a perfectly oval face and a long graceful neck. Her eldest sister had thickly fringed chocolate brown eyes, a classical straight nose, a wide sensuous mouth, and a model-like figure that made everything she wore look right.

Her gaze moved mockingly to Sue who was almost as tall but more lushly feminine, round curves everywhere topped by a pretty face, sparkling amber eyes and soft, honey-coloured curls that rippled down to her shoulders.

Lastly she looked derisively at Diana, a beautiful blue-eyed blonde who turned heads everywhere she went, her long hair straight and smooth like a curtain of silk, her lovely face always perfectly made up, her tall slim figure invariably enhanced by fabulous designer clothes. Easy for her to catch the eye of *her* boss. He'd have to be blind not to appreciate what an asset she was to him.

Next to her sisters Liz felt small, and not just because she was only average height and had what could be called a petite figure. She felt small in every sense. Her hair was a mousy colour and far too thick to manage easily. It did swamp her. Not only that, her eyes were a murky hazel, no clear colour at all, there was a slight bump in her nose, and her cheekbones and chinline *were* sharply angular. In fact, her only saving grace was good straight teeth.

At least, people said she had a nice smile. But she didn't feel like smiling right now. She felt utterly miserable. 'It's ridiculous to pretend I could be a knockout,' she stated bitingly. 'The only thing I've got going for me is a smart brain that keeps me in a good job, and it's been my experience that most men don't like too much smart in their women when it comes to personal relationships.'

'A smart man does, Liz,' her mother said quietly.

'And Cole Pierson is incredibly smart,' Diana quickly tagged on. 'He'd definitely value you on that score.'

'Would you please leave my boss out of this?' Liz almost stamped her foot in frustration at her younger sister's one-track mind. Any intimate connection with Cole was an impossible dream, for dozens of reasons.

'Regardless of your boss, Liz,' Jayne said in a serious vein. 'I truly think a makeover is a good idea. You're not plain. You've just never made the most of yourself. With some jazzy clothes and a new hairdo…'

'A lovely rich shade of red would do wonders for your hair,' Sue came in decisively. 'If you had it cut and layered to shape in just below your ears, it could look fantastic. Your skin is pale enough for red to look great with it and such a positive contrast would bring out the green in your eyes.'

'They're not green!' Liz cried in exasperation. 'They're…'

'More green than amber,' Sue judged. 'Red would definitely do the trick. Let me make an appointment with my hairdresser for you and I'll come along to advise.'

'And I can take you shopping. Outfit you in some smashing clothes,' Diana eagerly tagged on.

'At a discount price,' Jayne leapt in. 'Right, Diana? Not making it too frightfully expensive?'

'Right!'

'Hair first, clothes second,' Sue ordered.

'A visit to a beautician, too. Get the make-up right to match the new hair.'

'And accentuate the green in her eyes.'

'Don't forget shoes. Liz has got to get out of those matronly shoes.'

'Absolutely. Shapely legs should be shown off.'

'Not to mention a finely turned ankle.'

They all laughed, happy at the thought of getting their hands on their little sister and waving some magic wand that would turn her into one of them. Except it couldn't really happen, and as her sisters continued to rave on with their makeover plan, bouncing off each other, meaning well…she knew they *meant well*…Liz found herself on the verge of tears.

'Stop! Please stop!' she burst out, slamming her hands onto the island bench to gain their undivided attention. 'I'm me, okay? Not a doll for you to dress up. I'm okay as me. And I'll live my life my own way.'

The shaking vehemence in her voice shocked them

into silence. They stared at her, hurt showing on their faces at the blanket rejection of their ideas. They didn't understand where she was coming from, had never understood what it was like to be *her,* the odd one out amongst them. The tears pricked her eyes, threatening to start spilling.

'I'd like some time alone with Liz.'

Her mother's quiet demand floated over Liz's shoulder. She was still at the sink, wiping it back to its usual pristine state. Without a word of protest, her other three daughters got to their feet and trooped out to the patio. Liz turned to her mother, who slowly set the dishcloth aside, waiting for the absolute privacy she'd asked for, not turning until the others were gone.

Having screwed herself up for more talking, Liz was totally undone when her mother looked at her with sad, sympathetic understanding. Impossible to blink back the tears. Then her mother's arms were around her in a comforting hug and her head was being gently pressed onto a shoulder that had always been there for her to lean on in times of strife and grief.

'Let it out, Liz,' her mother softly advised. 'You've held in too much for too long.'

Control collapsed. She wept, releasing the bank of bad feelings that had been building up ever since Brendan had rejected all she'd offered him, preferring to be somewhere else.

'He wasn't right for you,' her mother murmured when the storm of tears eased. 'I know you tried to make him right for you, but he was never going to be, Liz. He's footloose and rootless and you like to be grounded.'

'But I did enjoy the travelling with him, Mum,' she protested.

'I'm sure you did, but it was also a way of going off independently, not competing with your sisters. You may not think of it like that, but being different for the sake of being different is not the answer. By attaching yourself to Brendan, you virtually shut them out of your life. They want back in, Liz. They want to help you. They're your sisters and they love you.'

She lifted her head, looking her mother in the eye. 'But I'm not like them.'

'No, you have your own unique individuality.' Her mouth curved into a tender, loving smile. 'My one brilliant daughter.'

Liz grimaced. 'Not so brilliant. Though I am good at my job.'

Her mother nodded. 'That's not the problem, is it? You're not feeling good about yourself as a woman. I don't think you have for a long time, Liz. It's easy to sweep away your sisters' makeover plan as some kind of false facade, but you could treat it as fun. A new look. A new style. It might very well give you a lift. Don't see it as competing with them. See it as something new for you.'

'You're urging me to be their guinea pig?'

This drew a chiding shake of the head. 'They're proud of your career in high finance, Liz. They admire your success there. How about conceding that they have expertise in fields you've ignored?'

She winced at the pointed reminder that in the feminine stakes, her sisters certainly shone and undoubtedly had an eye for things she hadn't bothered with. 'I guess they do know what they're talking about.'

'And then some,' her mother said dryly.

Liz sighed, giving in more because she was bereft of any plans for herself than in any belief that her life could be instantly brightened, along with her hair. 'Well, I don't suppose it will hurt.'

'You could be very pleasantly surprised. Jayne is right. You're not plain, Liz. You're just different.' Her mother patted her cheek encouragingly. 'Now go and make peace with them. Letting them have their way could be a very positive experience for all of you.'

'Okay. But if Diana thinks a new me will make any difference to Cole Pierson, she's dreaming.'

Her boss occupied a different planet.

A chilly one.

Even fiery red hair wasn't about to melt the ice in that man's veins. Or make him suddenly see her as a desirable woman. Why would he anyway, when he'd had Tara Summerville—a top-line international model—as his wife? Even Diana wasn't in that class.

A totally impossible dream.

CHAPTER TWO

His mother was upset.

Cole didn't like his mother being upset. It had taken her quite a while to get over his father's death and establish a life on her own. For the past few years she'd been happy, planning overseas trips and going on them with her bridge partner, Joyce Hancock, a retired school principal who was a natural organiser, a person he could trust to look after his mother on their travels. As misfortune would have it, Joyce had fallen and broken her hip so the tour they'd booked to South-East Asia had to be cancelled.

He'd spent the whole weekend trying to distract his mother with his company, cheer her up, but she'd remained down in the dumps, heaving miserable sighs, looking forlorn. Now, driving her back to her Palm Beach home after visiting Joyce in Mona Vale Hospital, Cole saw she was fighting tears. He reached across and squeezed her hand, trying to give sympathetic comfort.

'Don't worry about Joyce. Hip replacement is not a dangerous procedure,' he assured her. 'She'll be up and about soon enough.'

'She's annoyed with me for not going ahead with the trip by myself. But I don't want to go on my own.'

Unthinkable to Cole's mind. His mother would undoubtedly get flustered over the tour schedule, leave things in the hotel rooms, be at the wrong place at the wrong time. She'd become quite fluffy-headed in her widowhood, not having to account to anyone anymore, just floating along while Cole took care of any problems that were troublesome. He saw to the maintenance of her far too large but beloved home and looked after her finances. It was easier than trying to train her into being more responsible for herself.

'It's your choice, Mum. Joyce probably feels guilty about disappointing you,' he soothed.

She shook her head dejectedly. 'I'm disappointing her. She's right about *The Captain's Choice Tour Company*. Their people do look after everything for you. They even take a doctor along in case anyone gets sick or injured. Joyce wants me to go so I can tell her all about it. She says I'll meet people I can talk to. Make new friends...'

'That's easy for her to say,' Cole said dryly, knowing Joyce was the kind of person who'd bulldose her way into any company and feel right at home with it. His mother was made of more fragile stuff.

Her hands twisted fretfully. 'Maybe I should go. Nothing's been cancelled yet. I was going to do it tomorrow.'

Clearly she was torn and would feel miserable either way. 'You need a companion, Mum,' Cole stated categorically. 'You'll feel lost on your own.'

'But there's no one in our social circle who's free to take up Joyce's booking.'

He frowned at this evidence of her actively trying to find someone congenial to travel with. 'You really want to go?'

'I've been looking forward to it for so long. Though without Joyce…' Her voice wavered uncertainly.

Cole made a decision. It meant a sacrifice on his part. Liz Hart had been on vacation for the past two weeks and her fill-in had tested his tolerance level to the limit. He hated doing without his efficient personal assistant. Nevertheless, when it came to entrusting the management of his mother to someone else, he couldn't think of anyone better. No hitches with Liz Hart.

'I'll arrange for my P.A. to take up Joyce's booking and accompany you on the tour,' he said, satisfied that he'd come up with the perfect solution, both for his mother's pleasure and his peace of mind.

It jolted her out of her gloom. 'You can't do that, Cole.'

'Yes, I can,' he asserted. 'I'll put it to Liz first thing in the morning. I'm sure she'll agree.'

'I don't even know the girl!' his mother cried in shocked protest.

'You can come into the city tomorrow and I'll set up a lunch meeting. If you approve of her…fine. If you don't, I'm afraid the trip will be off.'

The lure of the tour clearly held a lot of weight. After a few moments, his mother gave in to curiosity. 'What's she like…this personal assistant of yours?'

'She's the kind of person who can handle anything I throw at her,' he replied, smiling confidently.

'Well, she'd have to be, wouldn't she, to keep up with you, Cole,' came the dryly knowing comment. 'I meant…what is she like as a person?'

He frowned, not quite sure how to answer. 'She fits in,' was the most appropriate description he could come up with.

This earned an exasperated roll of the eyes. 'What does she look like?'

'Always neat and tidy. Professional.'

'How old is she?'

'Not sure. Late twenties, I guess. Maybe early thirties.'

'What colour are her eyes?'

He didn't know, couldn't recall ever noticing. 'What does eye colour have to do with anything?'

His mother sighed. 'You just don't look, do you? Not interested. You've closed off all involvement with anyone. You've got to get past this, Cole. You're still a young man.'

He gritted his teeth, hating any reference to all he'd put behind him. 'Her eyes are bright.' he answered tersely. 'They shine with intelligence. That's more important to me than colour.'

The blank look her temporary fill-in had given him too many times over the past fortnight had filled him with frustration. He'd have to second someone else to take Liz Hart's place while she was off with his mother.

'Is she attractive…pretty…big…slight…tall… short…?'

Cole sighed over his mother's persistence on irrelevant detail. 'She's ordinary average,' he said impatiently. 'And always obliging, which is the main point here. Liz will ensure you have a trouble-free tour, Mum. No worries.'

His mother sighed. 'Do try to tell me more about her, Cole.'

She should be satisfied with what he'd already told her but he stretched his mind to find some pertinent point. 'She likes travel. Spends most of her time off travelling somewhere or other. I expect she'll jump at the chance of accompanying you to South-East Asia.'

'Then it won't be a completely burdensome chore for her, escorting me around?'

'Of course not. I wouldn't load you with a sour-puss. I'm sure you'll find Liz Hart a delight to be with.'

'Do you?'

'Do I what?'

'Find her a delight to be with.'

'Well, I'll certainly miss her,' he said with feeling.

'Ah!'

He glanced sharply at his mother. Her 'Ah!' had carried a surprising depth of satisfaction, making him wonder what she was thinking.

She smiled at him. 'Thank you, Cole. You're quite wonderful at fixing things for me. I'll look forward to meeting your Liz tomorrow.'

'Good!'

Problem solved.

His mother wasn't upset anymore.

Monday morning...

Cole heard Liz Hart arrive in the office which ad-joined his—promptly at eight-thirty as she did every workday. Totally reliable, he thought with satisfaction.

He had not qualms whatsoever about entrusting his mother's well-being and pleasure in this upcoming South-East Asia tour to his punctual and efficient personal assistant.

It didn't occur to him that the request he was about to make was tantamount to inviting Liz Hart into his personal and private life. To his mind it was simply a matter of moving people into position to achieve what had to be achieved. He could manage another two weeks more or less by himself, asking the absolute minimum of another temporary P.A., while his mother enjoyed a stress-free trip. Once the fortnight was over, everything would shift back to normal.

He rose from his desk and strode to the connecting door, intent on handing the tour folder to Liz so she could get straight to work on doing what had to be done to become Joyce Hancock's replacement. In his business, time was money and his time was too valuable to waste on extraneous matters. Liz would undoubtedly see to everything required of her—passport, visas, whatever.

He opened the door to find some stranger hanging her bag and coat on Liz's hatstand, taking up personal space that didn't belong to her. Cole frowned at the unexpected vision of a startling redhead, dressed in a clingy green sweater and a figure-hugging navy skirt with a split up the back—quite a distracting split, leading his gaze down a pair of finely shaped legs encased in sheer navy stockings, to pointedly female high-heeled shoes.

Who was this woman? And what did she think she was doing, taking up Liz's office? He hadn't been informed that his P.A. had called in, delaying her scheduled return to work. Unexplained change was not acceptable, especially when it entailed having someone foisted on him without his prior approval.

His gaze had travelled back up the curve of thigh and hip to the indentation of a very small waist before the unwelcome intruder turned around. Then he found himself fixated on very nicely rounded breasts, emphatically outlined by the soft, sexy sweater, with more attention being drawn to them by a V-neckline ending in a looped tie that hung down the valley of her cleavage.

'Good morning, Cole.'

The brisk, cool greeting stunned him with its familiarity. His gaze jerked up to an unfamiliar mouth, painted as brightly red as the thick cropped hair that flared out in waves and curls on either side of her face. The eyes hit a chord with him—very bright eyes—but even they looked different, bigger than they normally were and more sparkly. This wasn't the Liz Hart he was used to. Only her voice was instantly recognisable.

'What the devil have you done to yourself?' The words shot out, driven by a sense of aggrievement at the shock she'd given him.

A firmly chiseled chin which he'd previously thought of as strong, steady and determined, now tilted up in provocative challenge. 'I beg your pardon?'

He was distracted by the gold gypsy hoops dangling from her earlobes. 'This is not you, dammit!' he grated, his normal equilibrium thrown completely out of kilter by these changes in the person who worked most closely with him, a person he counted on not to rock his boats in any sense whatsoever.

Her eyes flashed a glittery warning. 'Are you objecting to my appearance?'

Red alert signals went off in his brain…sexual discrimination…harrassment…Liz was calling him on something dangerous here and he'd better watch his step. However disturbingly different she looked today, he knew she had a core of steel and would stand up for herself against anything she considered unreasonable or unjust.

'No,' he said decisively, taking firm control over the runaway reactions to an image he didn't associate with her. 'Your appearance is fine. It's good to have you back, Liz.'

'Thank you.' Her chin levelled off again, fighting mode discarded. She smiled. 'It's good to be back.'

This should have put them on the correct footing but Cole couldn't help staring at her face, which somehow lit up quite strikingly with the smile. Maybe it was the short fluffy red hair that made her smile look even whiter and her eyes brighter. Or the bright red lipstick. Whatever it was, she sure didn't look average ordinary anymore.

He wanted to ask…why the change? What had happened to her? But that was personal stuff he knew he shouldn't get into. He liked the parameters of their business relationship the way they were. Right now they felt threatened, without inviting further infringements on them.

He had to stop staring. Her cheeks were glowing pink, highlighting bones that now seemed to have an exotic, angular tilt. They must have always been like that. It made him feel stupid not to have noticed before. Had she been deliberately playing herself down during business hours, hiding her surprisingly feminine figure in unisex suits, keeping her hair plain and quiet, wearing only insignificant make-up?

'Is that something for me to deal with?' she asked, gesturing to the folder he was holding.

Conscious that his awkward silence had driven her to take some initiative, he didn't stop to reconsider the proposition he'd prepared. 'Yes,' he said, gratefully seizing on the business in hand. 'I need you to go to South-East Asia with my mother,' he blurted out.

She stared at him, shocked disbelief in her eyes.

Good to serve it right back to her, Cole thought, stepping forward and slapping the folder down on her desk, a buzz of adrenalin shooting through him at regaining control of the situation.

'It's all in here. The Captain's Choice Tour. Borneo, Burma, Nepal, Laos, Vietnam, Cambodia—all in fifteen days by chartered Qantas jet, leaving on Saturday week. You'll require extra passport photos for visas and innoculation shots for typhoid, hepatitis, and other diseases. You'll see the medical check list. I take it you have a usable passport?'

'Yes,' she answered weakly.

'Good! No problem then.'

She seemed frozen on the spot, still staring at him, not moving to open the folder. He tapped it to draw her attention to it.

'All the tickets are in here. Everything's been paid

for. You'll find them issued in the name of Joyce Hancock and first thing to do is notify the tour company that you'll be travelling in her place.'

'Joyce Hancock,' she repeated dazedly.

'My mother's usual travelling companion. Broke her hip. Can't go. None of her other friends can take the trip at such short notice,' he explained.

Liz Hart shook her head, the red hair rippling with the movement like a live thing that wasn't under any control. Very distracting. Cole frowned, realising she was indicating a negative response. Which was unacceptable. He was about to argue the position when she drew in a deep breath and spoke.

'Your mother...Mrs. Pierson...she doesn't even know me.'

'*I* know you. I've told her she'll be safe with you.'

'But...' She gestured uncertainly.

'Primarily my mother needs a manager on this trip. I have absolute faith in your management skills, not to mention your acute sense of diplomacy, tact, understanding, and generally sharp intelligence. Plus you're an experienced traveller.' He raised a challenging eyebrow. 'Correct?'

Another deep breath, causing a definite swell in the mounds under the clingy sweater which was a striking jewel green, somewhere between jade and emerald, a rich kind of medieval colour. The fanciful thought jolted Cole. He had to get his mind off her changed appearance.

'Thank you. It's nice to have my...attributes... appreciated,' she said in a somewhat ironic tone that sounded unsure of his end purpose. 'However, I do think I should meet with your mother...'

'Lunch today. Book a table for the three of us at Level 21. Twelve-thirty. My mother will join us there. She is looking forward to meeting you.'

'Is Mrs. Pierson…unwell?'

'Not at all. A bit woolly-headed about directions in strange places and not apt at dealing with time changes and demanding schedules, but perfectly sane and sound. She'll lean on you to get things right for her. That's your brief. Okay?'

'She's…happy…about this arrangement?'

'Impossible for her to go otherwise and she wants to go.'

'I see. You want me to be her minder.'

'Yes. I have every confidence in your ability to provide the support she needs to fully enjoy this trip.'

'What if she doesn't like me?'

'What's *not* to like?' he threw back at her more snappishly than he'd meant to, irritatingly aware that his mother would think this new version of Liz Hart was just lovely. And she would undoubtedly mock his judgment at having called his P.A. ordinary average.

No answer from Liz. Of course, it would be against her steely grain to verbally put herself down. Which increased the mystery of why she had *played* herself down physically these past three years. Had it been a feminist thing, a negation of her sexuality because she wanted her intellect valued?

Why had she suddenly decided to flaunt femininity now?

Dammit! He didn't have time to waste on such vagaries.

He tapped the folder again. 'I can leave this with you? No problems about dealing with it?' His eyes locked onto hers with the sharp demand of getting what he expected.

'No problems I can see,' she returned with flinty pride.

Her eyes were green.

With gold speckles around the rim.

'Fine! Let me know if you run into any.'

He stalked off into his own office, annoyed at how he was suddenly noticing every detail about a woman who'd been little more than a mind complementing his up until this morning. It was upsetting his comfort zone.

Why did she have to change?

It didn't feel right.

Just as well she was going off with his mother for two weeks. It would give him time to adjust to the idea of having his P.A. looking like a fiery sexpot. Meanwhile, he had work to do and he was not about to be distracted from it. Bad enough that he had to take time off for the lunch with his mother, which was bound to be another irritation because of Liz Hart's dramatic transformation.

Bad start to the morning.

Bad, bad, bad.

At least the food at Level 21 was good.

Though he'd probably choke on it, watching his mother being dazzled by her new travelling companion. No way was *she* going to be upset by a *colourful* Liz Hart, which was some consolation, but since he was decidedly upset himself, Cole wasn't sure that balanced the scales.

CHAPTER THREE

LIZ took a deep, deep breath, let it out slowly, then forced her feet to walk steadily to her desk, no teetering in the high-heels, shoulders back, correct carriage, just as Diana had drilled her. It was good to sit down. She was still quaking inside from the reaction her new image had drawn from Cole Pierson.

Diana had confidently predicted it would knock his socks off but Liz had believed he would probably look at her blankly for a few seconds, dismiss the whole thing as frivolous female foibles, then get straight down to business. Never, in a million years, would she have anticipated being *attacked* on it. Nor looked at so...so *intensely*.

It had been awful, turning around from the hatstand and finding those piercing blue eyes riveted on her breasts. Her heart had started galloping. Even worse, she'd felt her nipples hardening into prominent nubs, possibly becoming visible underneath the snug fit of the cashmere sweater.

She'd clipped out a quick greeting to get his focus off her body, only to have him stare at her mouth as though alien words had come out of it. Even when he had finally lifted his gaze to hers, she'd been totally rattled by the force of his concentration on how she looked. Which, she readily conceded, was vastly different to what he was used to, but certainly not warranting the outburst that came. Nor the criticism it implied.

Her own fierce response to it echoed through her mind now—*I will not let him make me feel wrong. Not on any grounds.*

There was no workplace law to say a woman couldn't change the colour of her hair, couldn't change the style of her clothes, couldn't touch up her make-up. It wasn't as if she'd turned up with hair tortured into red or blue or purple spikes or dreadlocks. Red was a natural hair colour and the short layered style was what she'd call conservative modern, not the least bit outlandish. Her clothes were perfectly respectable and her make-up appropriate—certainly not overdone—to match the new colouring.

In fact, no impartial judge would say her appearance did not fit the position she held. All her sisters had declared she was now perfectly put together and Liz herself had ended up approving the result of their combined efforts. Her mother was right. It did make her feel good to look brighter and more stylish. She'd even started smiling at herself in the mirror.

And she wasn't about to let Cole Pierson wipe *that* smile off her face, just because he'd feel more comfortable if she merged into the office furniture again so he could regard her as another one of his computers. Though he had attributed her with management skills, diplomacy, tact, understanding, and sharp intelligence, which did put her a few points above a computer. And amazingly, he trusted her enough to put his mother into her keeping!

Having burned off her resentment at her boss's totally intemperate remarks on what was none of his business, Liz focused on the folder he'd put on her desk. Surprises had come thick and fast this morning. Apart from Cole's taking far too much *physical* notice of her, she had been summarily appointed guardian to a woman she'd never met, and handed a free trip to South-East Asia, no doubt travelling first-class all the way on The Captain's Choice Tour.

Right in the middle of this, Cole had listed Nepal amongst the various destinations.

Brendan was in Nepal.

Not that there was any likelihood of meeting up with him, and she didn't really want to…did she? What was finished was finished. But there was a somewhat black irony in her going there, too. Especially in not doing everything on the cheap, as Brendan would have to.

You can do better than Brendan Wheeler, her mother had said with a conviction that had made Liz feel she had settled for less than she should in considering a life partner.

Maybe her mother was right.

In any event, this trip promised many better things than bunking down in backpacker hostels.

On the front of The Captain's Choice folder was printed 'The leader in luxury travel to remote and exotic destinations.' Excitement was instantly ignited. She opened the folder and read all about the itinerary, delighted anticipation zooming at the places she would be visiting, and all in a deluxe fashion.

The accommodation was fantastic—The Hyatt Regency Hotel in Kathmandu, The Opera Hilton in

Hanoi, a 'Raffles' hotel in Phnom Penh. No expense spared anywhere…a chartered flight over Mount Everest, and a chartered helicopter to Halong Bay in Vietnam, another chartered flight to the ancient architectural wonder of Angkor Wat in Cambodia, even a specially chartered steam train to show them some of the countryside in Burma.

She could definitely take a lot of this kind of travel. No juggling finances, no concern over how to get where, no worry about making connections, no trying to find a decent meal…it was all laid out and paid for.

Even if Cole's mother was a grumpy battleaxe, Liz figured it couldn't be too hard to win her over by being determinedly cheerful. After all, Mrs. Pierson had to want this trip very much to agree to her son's plan, so mutual enjoyment should be reached without too much trouble.

Tact, diplomacy, understanding…Liz grinned to herself as she reached for the telephone, ready now to get moving on sealing her place for this wonderful new adventure. Her changed appearance had probably knocked Cole's socks off this morning, though in a more negative way than Diana had plotted, but he had still paid her a huge compliment by giving her this extra job with his mother. Better than a bonus.

It made her feel good.

Really good.

She zinged through the morning, booking the table at Level 21—no problem to fit Cole Pierson's party in at short notice since he regularly used the restaurant for business lunches—then lining up everything necessary for her to take Joyce Hancock's place on the tour.

Cole did not reappear. He did not call her, either. He remained secluded in his own office, no doubt tending meticulously to his own business. At twelve-fifteen, Liz went to the Ladies' Room to freshen up, smiled at herself in the mirror, determined that nothing her boss said or did would unsettle her again, then proceeded to beard the lion in his den, hoping he wouldn't bite this time.

She gave a warning knock on the door, entered his office, waited for him to look up from the paperwork on his desk, ignored the frown, and matter-of-factly stated, 'It's time to leave if we're to meet your mother at twelve-thirty.'

Since Cole's financial services company occupied a floor of the Chifley Tower, one of the most prestigious buildings in the city centre, all they had to do was catch an elevator up to Level 21, which, of course, was also one of Sydney's most prestigious restaurants. This arrangement naturally suited Cole's convenience, as well as establishing in his clients' minds that big money was made here and this location amply displayed that fact.

Cold blue eyes bored into hers for several nerve-jangling moments. He certainly knew how to put a chill in a room. Liz wondered if she should have put her suitcoat on, but they weren't going outside where there was a wintery bite in the air. This was just her boss, being his usual self, and it was good that he had returned to being his usual self.

Though as he rolled his big executive chair back

from his work station and rose to his full impressive height, Liz did objectively note that Sue was not wrong in calling him tall, dark and handsome, what with his thick black hair, black eyebrows, darkly toned skin, a strong male face, squarish jaw, firm mouth, straight nose, neat ears. And those piercing eyes gave him a commanding authority that accentuated his *presence*.

The Armani suits he invariably wore added to his presence, too. Cole Pierson had dominant class written all over him. Sometimes, it really piqued Liz. It didn't seem fair that anyone should have so much going for him. But then she told herself he wasn't totally human.

Although the robotic facade *had* cracked this morning.

Scary stuff.

Better not to think about it.

Move on, move on, move on, she recited, holding her breath as Cole moved towards her, mouth grim, eyes raking over her again, clearly not yet having come to terms with her brighter presence.

'Did you call up to see if my mother had arrived?' he rapped out.

'No. I considered it a courtesy that we be there on time.'

'My mother is not the greatest time-keeper in the world.' He paused beside Liz near the door. 'Which is why she needs you,' he rammed home with quite unnecessary force.

'All the more reason to show her I'm reliable on that point,' she retorted, and could have sworn he

breathed steam through his nostrils as he abruptly
waved her to precede him out of both of their offices.

It made Liz extremely conscious of walking with
straight-backed dignity. It was ridiculous, given his
icy eyes, that she felt the bare nape of her neck burning. He had to be watching her, which was highly
disconcerting because usually his whole attention was
claimed by whatever was working through his mind.
She didn't want his kind of intense focus trained on
her. It was like being under a microscope, making her
insides squirmish.

She breathed a sigh of relief when they finally entered the elevator and stood side by side in the compartment as it zoomed up to Level 21. Cole held his
hands loosely linked in front of them and watched the
numbers flashing over the door. It looked like a relaxed pose, but he emanated a tension that erased
Liz's initial relief.

Maybe he was human, after all.

Was it *her* causing this rift in his iron-like com-
posure, or the prospect of this meeting with his
mother?

This thought reminded Liz that *she* should be thinking about his mother, preparing herself to answer any
questions put to her in a positive and reassuring manner. Of course, her response depended largely on the
kind of person Cole's mother was. Liz hoped she
wasn't frosty. Cole had said fluffy, but that might only
mean her mind wasn't as razor-sharp as his.

Liz was fast sharpening her own mind as they were
met at the entrance to the restaurant by the maitre d'

and informed that Mrs. Pierson had arrived and was enjoying a drink in the bar lounge.

'Must be anxious,' Cole muttered as they were led to where a woman sat on a grey leather sofa, her attention drawn to the fantastic view over the city of Sydney, dramatically displayed by the wall of windows.

Her hair was pure white, waving softly around a slightly chubby face which was relatively unlined and still showing how pretty she must have been in her youth. About seventy, Liz judged, taking heart at the gentle, ladylike look of the woman. Definitely not a battleaxe. Not frosty, either. She wore a pink Chanel style suit with an ivory silk blouse, pearl brooch, pearl studs in her ears, and many rings on her fingers.

'Mum!'

Her son's curt tone whipped her head around, her whole body jerking slightly at being startled. Bright blue eyes looked up at him, then made an instant curious leap to Liz. Her mouth dropped open in sheer surprise.

'Mum!' Cole said again, the curt tone edged with vexation now.

Her mouth shut into a line of total exasperation and she gave him a look that seemed to accuse him of being absolutely impossible and in urgent need of having his head examined.

Liz thought she heard Cole grind his teeth. However, he managed to unclench them long enough to say, 'This is my P.A., Liz Hart…my mother, Nancy Pierson.'

Nancy rose to her feet, her blue eyes glittering with

a frustration that spilled into speech as she held out her hand to Liz. 'My dear, how *do* you put up with him?'

Tact and diplomacy were right on the line here!

'Cole is the best boss I've ever had,' Liz declared with loyal fervour. 'I very much enjoy working with him.'

'Work!' Nancy repeated in a tone of disgust. 'Tunnel vision…that's what he's got. Sees nothing but work.'

'Mum!' Thunder rolled through Cole's warning protest.

Liz leapt in to avert the storm. 'Cole did cover your trip to South-East Asia this morning, Mrs. Pierson.' She beamed her best smile and poured warmth into her voice as she added, 'Which I think is wonderful.'

It did the trick, drawing Nancy out of her grumps and earning a smile back. She squeezed Liz's hand in a rush of pleasure. 'Oh, I think so, too. Far too wonderful to miss.'

Liz squeezed back. 'I'm simply over the moon that Cole thought of me as a companion for you. Such marvellous places to see…'

'Well…' She gave her son an arch look that still had a chastening gleam. 'Occasionally he gets some things right.'

'A drink,' Cole bit out. 'Liz, something for you? Mum, a refill?'

'Just water, thank you,' Liz quickly answered.

'Champagne,' Nancy commanded, and suddenly there was a wickedly mocking twinkle in her eyes.

'I'm beginning to feel quite bubbly again, now that I've met your Liz, Cole.'

His Liz? Exactly what terms had Cole used to describe her to his mother? Nothing with a possessive sense, surely.

'I'm glad you're happy,' he said on an acid note and headed for the bar.

Nancy squeezed Liz's hand again before letting go and gesturing to the lounge. 'Come and sit down with me and let us get better acquainted.'

'What would you like to know about me?' Liz openly invited as she sank onto the soft leather sofa.

'Not about work,' came the decisive dismissal. 'Tell me about your family.'

'Well, my parents live at Neutral bay…'

'Nice suburb.'

'Dad's a doctor. Mum was a nurse but…'

'She gave it up when the family came along.'

'Yes. Four daughters. I'm the third.'

'My goodness! That must have been a very female household.'

Liz laughed. 'Yes. Dad always grumbled about being outvoted. But he now has three sons-in-law to stand shoulder to shoulder with him.'

'So your three sisters are married. How lovely! Nice husbands?'

Under Nancy's eager encouragement, Liz went on to describe her sisters' lives and had just finished a general rundown on them when Cole returned, setting the drinks down on the low table in front of them and dropping onto the opposite sofa. Into the lull following their 'thankyous,' Nancy dropped the one question Liz didn't want to answer.

'So what about your social life, Liz? Or are you like Cole...' a derisive glance at her son. '...not having one.'

It instantly conjured up the hole left by Brendan's defection. She delayed a reply, picking up the glass of water, fiercely wishing the question hadn't been asked, especially put as it had been, linking her to her boss who was listening.

Unexpectedly he came to her rescue. 'You're getting too personal, Mum,' he said brusquely. 'Leave it alone.'

Nancy aimed a sigh at him. 'Has it occurred to you, Cole, that such a bright, striking young woman could have a boyfriend who might not take kindly to her leaving him behind while she travels with me?'

He beetled an accusing frown at Liz as though this was all her fault, then sliced an impatient look at his mother. 'What objection could a boyfriend have? It's only for two weeks and you can hardly be seen as a rival.'

'It's short notice. The trip takes up three weekends. They might have prior engagements,' came the ready arguments. 'Did you even ask this morning, or did you simply go into command mode, expecting Liz to carry through your plan, regardless?'

A long breath hissed through his teeth.

Liz felt driven to break in. 'Mrs. Pierson...'

'Call me Nancy, dear.'

'Nancy...' She tried an appeasing smile to cover the angst of her current single state. '...I don't have a boyfriend at the moment. I'm completely free to take up the amazingly generous opportunity Cole handed me this morning. I would have told him so if I wasn't.'

Tact, diplomacy…never mind that the hole was humiliatingly bared.

'Satisfied?' Cole shot at his mother.

She smiled back at him. 'Completely.' It was a surprisingly smug pronouncement, as though she had won the point.

Liz was lost in whatever byplay was going on between mother and son, but she was beginning to feel very much like the meat in the sandwich. Anxious to get the conversation focused back on the trip, she offered more relevant information about herself.

'I haven't been to Kuching but I have travelled to Malaysia before.'

Thankfully, Nancy seized on that prior experience and Liz managed to keep feeding their mutual interest in travel over lunch, skilfully smoothing over the earlier tension in their small party. Cole ate his food, contributing little to the table talk, though he did flash Liz a look of wry appreciation now and then, well aware she was working hard at winning over his mother.

Not that it was really hard. Nancy seemed disposed to like her, the blue eyes twinkling pleasure and approval in practically everything Liz said. Oddly enough, Liz was more conscious of her boss watching and listening, and whenever their eyes met, the understanding that flashed between them gave her heart a little jolt.

This had never happened before and she tried to analyse why now? Because his mother made this more personal than business? Because he was looking at her from a different angle, seeing the woman behind the P.A.? Because she was doing the same thing, seeing him as Nancy's son instead of the boss?

It was confusing and unsettling.

She didn't want to feel…*touched*…by this man, or close to him in any emotional sense. No doubt he'd freeze her out again the moment this meeting with his mother was over.

'Now, are you free this Saturday, my dear?' Nancy inquired once coffee was served.

'Yes?' Liz half queried, wondering what else was required of her.

'Good! You must come over to my home at Palm Beach and check my packing. Joyce always does that for me. It eliminates doubling up on things, taking too much. Do you have a car? It's difficult to get to by public transport. If you don't have a car…'

Liz quickly cut in. 'Truly, it won't be a problem. I'll manage.'

She'd never owned a car. No need when public transport was not only faster into the city, but much, much cheaper than running a car. Palm Beach was, however, a fair distance out, right at the end of the northern peninsula, but she'd get there somehow.

'I was going to say Cole could bring you.' She smiled at her son. 'You could, dear, couldn't you? Don't forget you're meeting with the tradesman who's going to quote for the new paving around the pool on Saturday.' She frowned. 'I think he said eleven o'clock. Or was it one o'clock?'

Cole sighed. 'I'll be there, Mum. And I'll collect and deliver Liz to you,' he said in a tone of sorely tried patience.

Oh, great! Liz thought, preferring the cost of a taxi to being a forced burden loaded onto her boss's shoulders. But clearly she wasn't going to get any say in this so she might as well grin and bear it. Though she doubted Cole would find a grin appropriate. He was indulging his mother but the indulgence was wearing very, very thin.

'You'd better come early. Before eleven,' Nancy instructed, then smiled at Liz. 'We'll have a nice lunch together. I've so enjoyed this one. And, of course, we have to be sure we've got all the right clothes for our trip.'

Liz had been thinking cargo pants and T-shirts for daywear and a few more stylish though still casual outfits for dinner at night, but she held her tongue, not knowing what Nancy expected of her. She would see on Saturday.

A great pity Cole had to be there.

He was probably thinking the same thing about her.

In fact, Liz wondered if Nancy Pierson was deliberately putting the two of them together to somehow score more points off her son. She might be fluffy-headed about time, but Liz suspected she was as sharp as a tack when it came to people. And she was looking smug again.

'Everything settled to your satisfaction, Mum?' Cole dryly inquired.

'Yes.' She smiled sweetly at him. 'Thank you, dear. I'm sure I'll have a lovely time with your Liz. So good of you to give her to me. I imagine you'll be quite lost without her.'

'No one is indispensable.'

A chill ran down Liz's spine. She threw an alarmed look at Cole, frightened that she'd somehow put her job on the line by courting his mother. The last thing she wanted at this uncertain point in her life was to lose the position that gave her the means to move on.

Cole caught the look and frowned at the flash of vulnerability. 'Though I must admit it's very difficult to find anyone who can remotely fill Liz's shoes as my P.A.,' he stated, glowering at her as though she should know that. 'In fact, I may very well take some time off work while she's away to save myself the aggravation.'

Both Liz and Nancy stared at him in stunned disbelief.

Cole taking time off work was unheard of. He ate, drank, and slept work.

Surprises were definitely coming thick and fast today!

The best one, Liz decided with a surge of tingling pleasure, was the accumulating evidence that Cole Pierson really valued her. That made her feel better than good. It made her feel...*extra special.*

CHAPTER FOUR

COLE had expected Liz Hart to manage his mother brilliantly. That had never been in doubt. However, while the meeting had achieved his purpose—his mother happily accepting his P.A. as her companion for the trip—there were other outcomes that continued to niggle at his mind, making the rest of Monday afternoon a dead loss as far as any productive work was concerned.

Firstly, his mother considered him a blind idiot.

That was Liz's fault.

Secondly, his mother had neatly trapped him into some ridiculous matchmaking scheme, forcibly coupling him with Liz on Saturday.

While he couldn't entirely lay the blame for that at his P.A.'s door, if she hadn't completely changed how she looked, his mother wouldn't have been inspired to plot this extraneous togetherness.

Thirdly, what had happened to the boyfriend? While Cole had never met the man in Liz Hart's life and not given him a thought this morning, he had been under the impression there was a long-running relationship. The name, Brendan, came to mind. Certainly on the few occasions Liz had spoken of personal travel plans, she'd used the plural pronoun. 'We...'

Had she lied to put a swift end to the fuss his

mother had made? Surely insisting her boyfriend wouldn't object could have achieved the same end.

Cole wanted that point cleared up.

Maybe the departure of the boyfriend had triggered the distracting metamorphosis from brown moth to bright butterfly.

Lastly, why would Liz feel insecure about her job? She had every reason to feel confident about holding her position. He'd never criticised her work. She had to know how competent she was. It was absurd of her to look afraid when he'd said no one was indispensable.

The whole situation with her today had been exasperating and continued to exasperate even after she left to go home. Cole resolved to shut it all out of his mind tomorrow. And for the rest of the working week. Perhaps on the drive to his mother's house on Saturday he'd get these questions answered, clear up what was going on in Liz's head. Then he'd feel comfortable around her again.

On Tuesday morning she turned up in a slinky leopard print outfit that totally wrecked his comfort zone, giving him the sense of a jungle cat prowling around him with quiet, purposeful manoeuvres. She also wore sexy bronze sandals with straps that crisscrossed up over her ankles, making him notice how fine-boned they were.

Wednesday she gave the tight navy skirt with the slit up the back a second wearing, but this time topped with a snug cropped jacket in vibrant violet, an unbelievably stunning combination with the red hair. Cole found his gaze drawn to it far too many times.

Thursday came the leopard print skirt with a black sweater, and the gold hoop earrings that dangled so distractingly. *Striking,* his mother had said, and it was a disturbingly apt description. Cole was struck by thoughts he hadn't entertained for a long time. If Liz Hart was free of any attachment…but mixing business with pleasure was always a mistake. Stupid to even be tempted.

Friday fueled the temptation. She wore a bronze button-through dress which wasn't completely buttoned through, showing provocative flashes of leg. A wide belt accentuated her tiny waist, the stand-up collar framed her vivid hair and face, and the strappy bronze sandals got to him again. The overall effect was very sexy. In fact, the more he thought about Liz Hart, the more he thought she comprised a very desirable package.

But best to leave well enough alone.

He wasn't ready for a serious relationship and an office affair would inevitably undermine the smooth teamwork they'd established at work. Besides which, he reflected with considerable irony, Liz had not given any sign of seeing *him* in a sexual light. No ripple of disturbance in her usual efficiency.

She did seem to be smiling at him more often but he couldn't be sure that wasn't simply a case of the smile being more noticeable, along with her mouth, her eyes, and everything else about her. Nevertheless, the smile was getting to be insidious. More times than not he found himself smiling back, feeling a lingering pleasure in the little passage of warmth between them.

No harm in being friendly, he told himself, as long

as it didn't diminish his authority. After all, Liz had worked in relative harmony with him for three years. Though getting too friendly wouldn't do, either. A line had to be drawn. Business was business. A certain distance had to be kept.

That distance was clearly on Liz's mind when she entered his office at the end of their working week, and with an air of nervous tension, broached the subject—'About tomorrow…going to your mother's home at Palm Beach…'

'Ah, yes! Where and when to pick you up.'

Her hands picked fretfully at each other. 'You really don't have to.'

'Easier if I do.' Cole leaned back in his chair to show that he was relaxed about it.

'I've worked out the most efficient route by public transport. It's not a problem,' she assured him.

'It will be a problem for me if I arrive without you,' he drawled pointedly.

'Oh!' She grimaced, recalling the acrimony between mother and son. Her eyes flashed an anxious plea. 'I don't want to put you out, Cole.'

'It's my mother putting me out, not you. I don't mind obliging her tomorrow, Liz.' He reached for a notepad. 'Give me your address.'

More hand-picking. 'I could meet you somewhere on the way…'

'Your address,' he repeated, impatient with quibbling.

'It will be less hassle if…'

'Do you have a problem with giving me your address, Liz?' he cut in.

She winced. 'I live at Bondi Junction. It would mean your backtracking to pick me up…'

'Ten minutes at most from where I live at Benelong Point.'

'Then ten minutes back again before heading off in the right direction,' she reminded him.

'I think I can spare you twenty minutes.'

She sighed. 'I'd feel better about accepting a lift from you if we could meet on the way. I can catch a train to…'

'Are you worried that your boyfriend might object if I pick you up from your home?' The thought had slid into his mind and spilled into words before Cole realised it was openly probing her private life and casting himself in the role of a rival.

She stared at him, shocked at the implications of the question.

Cole was somewhat shocked at the indiscretion himself, but some belligerent instinct inside him refused to back down from it. The urge to know the truth of her situation had been building all week. He stared back, waiting for her answer, mentally commanding it.

A tide of heat flowed up her neck and burned across her cheekbones, making their slant more prominent and her eyes intensely bright. Cole was conscious of a fine tension running between them, a silent challenge emanating from her, striking an edge of excitement in him…the excitement of contest he always felt with a clash of wills, spurring on his need to win.

'I told you on Monday I don't have a boyfriend,' she bit out.

'No. You told my mother that, neatly ending her blast at me.'

'It's the truth.'

'Since when? The last I heard, just before you left on vacation, you had plans to travel with…is it Brendan?'

Her mouth compressed into a thin line of resistance.

'Who's been floating around in your background for as long as you've been working with me,' Cole pushed relentlessly. 'Probably before that, as well.'

'He's gone. I'm by myself now,' she said in defiant pride.

'Send him packing, did you?'

'He packed himself off,' she flashed back derisively.

'You're telling me he left you?'

'He didn't like my style of management.'

'Man's a fool.'

Her mouth tilted into a wry little smile. 'Thank you.'

No smile in her eyes, Cole noted. They looked bleak. She'd been hurt by the rejection of what she was, possibly hurt enough to worry about how rightly or wrongly she managed her job, hence the concern about losing it, too.

Satisfied that he now understood her position, Cole restated his. 'I shall pick you up at your home. Your address?'

She gave it without further argument, though her tone had a flat, beaten quality he didn't like. 'I was only trying to save you trouble,' she muttered, excusing her attempt to manage him.

'I appreciate the value you place on my time, Liz.' He finished writing down her address and looked up, wanting to make her feel valued. 'You're obliging my mother. The least I can do is save *you* some of your leisure time. Does ten o'clock suit?'

'Yes. Thank you.' Her cheeks were still burning but her hands had forgotten their agitation.

He smiled to ease the last of her tension. 'You're welcome. Just don't feel you have to indulge all my mother's whims tomorrow. Do only what's reasonable to you. Okay?'

She nodded.

He glanced at his watch. 'Time for you to leave to get those injections for the trip.' He smiled again. 'Off you go. I'll see you in the morning.'

'Thank you,' she repeated, looking confused by his good humour.

Cole questioned it himself once she left. He decided it had nothing to do with the fact she was free of any attachment. That was irrelevant to him. No, it was purely the satisfaction of having the mysteries surrounding her this week resolved. Even the change of image made sense. Given that Brendan was stupidly critical, no doubt she'd been suppressing her true colours for the sake of falling in with what he wanted.

Liz was well rid of that guy.

He'd obviously been dragging her down.

Cole ruefully reflected that was what his ex-wife had accused him of doing, though he'd come to recognise it had been easier to blame him than take any responsibility herself for the breakdown of their marriage. At the time he hadn't cared. All that had been good in their relationship had died…with their baby son.

For several moments the grief and guilt he'd locked away swelled out of the sealed compartment in his mind. He pushed them back. Futile feelings, achieving nothing. The past was past. It couldn't be changed. And there was work to be done.

He brought his concentration to bear on the figures listed on his computer monitor screen. He liked their logical patterns, always a reason for everything. Figures didn't lie or deceive or distort things. There were statiticians who used them to do precisely that, but figures by themselves had a pure truth. Cole was comfortable with figures.

He told himself he'd now be comfortable again with Liz Hart. It was all a matter of fitting everything into place—a straightforward pattern built on truth and logic. It wouldn't matter what she wore or how she looked tomorrow, he wouldn't find it distracting. It was all perfectly understandable.

As for the sexual attraction…a brief aberration.

No doubt it would wear off very quickly.

His desk telephone rang, evoking a frown of annoyance. No Liz to intercept and monitor his calls. He didn't talk to clients off the cuff, but it could be an in-house matter being referred to him. Hard to ignore the buzzing. He snatched up the receiver.

'Pierson.'

'Cole…finally,' came the distinctive voice of his almost ex-wife.

'Tara…' It was the barest of acknowledgments. He had nothing to say to her. An aggressive tension seized his entire body, an instinctive reaction to anything she might say to him.

'I tried to get hold of you all last weekend. You weren't at the penthouse…'

'I was with my mother at Palm Beach,' he cut in, resenting the tone that suggested he should still be at Tara's beck and call. She'd been *enjoying* the company of several other men since their separation, clearing him of any lingering sense of obligation to answer any of her needs.

'Your mother…' A hint of mockery in her voice.

It had been one bone of contention in their marriage that Cole spent too much time looking after his mother instead of devoting his entire attention to what Tara wanted, which was continual social activity in the limelight. Not even her pregnancy and the birth of their baby son had slowed her merry-go-round of engagements. If they hadn't been out at a party, leaving David in the care of his nanny…

'Get to the point, Tara,' he demanded, mentally blocking the well-worn and totally futile *if only* track in his mind.

She heaved a sigh at his bluntness, then in a sweetly cajoling tone, said, 'You do remember that our divorce becomes final next week…'

'The date is in my diary.'

'I thought we should get together and…'

'I believe our respective solicitors have covered

every piece of that ground,' he broke in tersely, angry at the thought that Tara was thinking of demanding even more than he had conceded to her in the divorce settlement.

'Darling, you've been more than generous, but…do we really want this?'

The hair on the back of his neck bristled. 'What do you mean?' he snapped.

She took a deep breath. 'You know I've been out and about with a few men since our separation, but the truth is…none of them match up to you, Cole. And I know you haven't formed a relationship with anyone else. I keep thinking if David hadn't died…'

His jaw clenched.

'It just affected everything between us. We both felt so bad…' Another deep breath. 'But time helps us get over these things. We had such a good life going for us, Cole. I was thinking we should give it another shot, at least try it for a while…'

'No!' The word exploded from him, driven by a huge force of negative feelings that were impossible to contain.

'Cole…we could try for another child,' she rolled on, ignoring his response, dropping her voice to a soft throaty purr that promised more than a child. 'Let's get together tomorrow and talk about it. We could have lunch at…'

'Forget it!' he bit out, hating what could only be a self-serving offer. Tara had never *really* wanted a child, hadn't cared enough about David to spend loving time with him. The nanny had done everything

Cole hadn't done himself for his son—the nanny who'd been more distraught than Tara when...

'I'll be lunching with Mum tomorrow,' he stated coldly, emphasising the fact he was not about to change any plans at this point. 'I won't be doing anything to stop the divorce going through. We reached the end of our relationship a long time ago, Tara, and I have no inclination whatsoever to revive it.'

'Surely a little reunion wouldn't hurt. If we could just talk...'

'I said forget it. I mean precisely that.'

He put the receiver down, switched off his computer, got up and strode out of the office, the urge for some intense, mind-numbing activity driving him to head for the private gymnasium where he worked out a couple of times a week.

He didn't want sex with his almost ex-wife.

It was sex that had drawn him into marrying Tara Summerville in the first place. Sex on legs. That was Tara. It had blinded him to everything else about her until well after the wedding. And there he'd been, trapped by a passionate obsession which had gradually waned under one disillusionment after another.

He might have held the marriage together for David's sake, but he certainly didn't want back in. No way. Never. If he ever married again it would be to someone like...he smiled ironically as Liz Hart popped into his mind.

Liz, who was valiantly trying to rise above being dumped by her long-term lover, revamping herself so effectively she'd stirred up feelings that Cole now recognised as totally inappropriate to both time and circumstance.

No doubt Liz was currently very vulnerable to being desired. It was probably the best antidote for the poison of rejection. But he was the wrong man in the wrong place to take advantage of the situation. She needed to count on him as her boss, not suddenly be presented with a side of him that had nothing to do with work.

Still the thought persisted that Liz Hart could be the perfect antidote to the long poisonous hangover from Tara.

Crazy idea.

Better work that out of his mind, too.

CHAPTER FIVE

FORTUNATELY, Liz wasn't kept waiting long at the medical centre. The doctor checked off the innoculations on the yellow card which went straight into the passport folder, along with the reissued tickets and all the other paperwork now acquired for the trip to South-East Asia. *Done,* Liz thought, and wished she was flying off tomorrow instead of having to accompany Cole Pierson to his mother's home.

It was quite scary how conscious she'd become of him as a man. All this time she'd kept him slotted under the heading of her boss—an undeniably male boss but the male part had only been a gender thing, not a sexual thing. This past week she'd found herself looking at him differently, reacting to him differently, even letting her mind dwell on how very attractive he was, especially when he smiled.

As she pushed through the evening peak hour commuter horde and boarded the train for Bondi Junction, she decided it had to be her sisters' fault, prompting her into reassessing Cole through their eyes. Though it was still a huge reach to consider him a possible marriage prospect. First would have to come…no, don't think about steps towards intimacy.

If her mind started wandering along those lines while she was riding with him in his car tomorrow, it could lead her into some dubious response or glance that Cole might interpret as trouble where he didn't want trouble. As it was, he was probably putting two and two together and coming up with a readily predictable answer—boyfriend gone plus new image equals man-hunting.

She would die if he thought for one moment she was hunting him. Because she wasn't. No way would she put her job at risk, which would certainly be the case if anything personal between them didn't work out. Bad enough that this trip with his mother had bared private matters that were changing the parameters of how they dealt with each other.

It didn't feel *safe* anymore.

It felt even less safe to have Cole Pierson coming to her home tomorrow, picking her up and bringing her back. Liz brooded over how he'd torpedoed her alternative plan, making the whole thing terribly personal by questioning her about Brendan and commenting on the aborted relationship.

She must have alighted from the train at Bondi Junction and walked to her apartment on automatic pilot, because nothing impinged on her occupied mind until she heard her telephone ringing in the kitchen.

It was Diana on the line. 'How did it go today?' Eager to hear some exciting result that would make all her efforts worthwhile.

'My arm is sore from the injections,' Liz replied, instinctively shying from revealing anything else.

'Oh, come on, Liz. That bronze dress was the pièce de résistance. It had to get a rise from him.'

'Well, he did notice it…' making her feel very self-conscious a number of times '…but he didn't *say* anything.'

Diana laughed. 'It's working. It's definitely working.'

'It might be angry notice, you know,' Liz argued. 'I told you how he reacted on Monday.'

'Pure shock. Which was what he needed to start seeing you in a different light. And don't worry about anger. Anger's good. Shows you've got to him.'

'But I'm not sure I want to get to him, Diana. It's been a very…uneasy…week.'

'No pain, no gain.'

Liz rolled her eyes at this flippant dictum. 'Look!' she cried in exasperation. 'It was different for you. A fashion buyer operates largely on her own, not under her boss's nose on a daily basis. There was room for you to pursue the attraction without causing any threat to your work situation.'

'You're getting yourself into a totally unnecessary twist, Liz. Cole Pierson is the kind of man who'll do the running. All you have to do is look great, say *yes,* and let things happen.'

'But what if…'

'Give that managing mind of yours a rest for once,' Diana broke in with a huff of impatience. 'Spontaneity is the key. Go with the flow and see where it takes you.'

To not being able to pay the mortgage if I lose my job, Liz thought. Yet there was something insidiously tempting about Diana's advice. She'd been *managing* everything for so long—*stifling* Brendan—and where had it got her?

On the discard shelf.

And Diana was right about Cole. He'd rolled right over the arrangements she'd tried to manage for tomorrow. If there was any running to be done, he'd certainly do it his way. Of course the choice to say yes or no was hers, but where either answer might lead was still very tricky.

'Maybe nothing will happen,' she said in her confusion over whether she wanted it to or not.

'He's taking you to a meeting with his mother tomorrow, isn't he?'

Liz wished she hadn't blabbed quite so much to Diana on Monday night. 'It's just about the trip,' she muttered.

'Wear the camel pants-suit with the funky tan hip belt and leave the top two buttons of the safari jacket undone,' came the marching orders.

'That's too obvious.' The three buttons left undone on her skirt today had played havoc with her nerves every time Cole had glanced down.

'No, it's not. It simply telegraphs the fact you're not buttoned up anymore. And use that *Red* perfume by Giorgio. It smells great on you.'

'I'm not good at this, Diana.'

'Just do as I say. Got to go now. Ward's arrived home. Good luck tomorrow and don't forget to smile a lot.'

Liz released a long, heavy sigh as she put the receiver down. This linking her up with Cole Pierson was turning into a personal crusade for her younger sister. Liz had tried to dampen it down, to no avail. She had the helter-skelter feeling that wheels had been set in motion on Monday and she had no control over where they were going.

At least she'd had little time to feel depressed over her single state. This weekend could have looked bleak and empty without Brendan. Instead of fretting over how to act with Cole, she should be grateful that the Piersons—mother and son—had filled up tomorrow for her.

Besides, she had Diana's instructions to follow and she carried them out to the letter the next morning, telling herself the outfit would undoubtedly please Nancy Pierson's sense of rightness. Classy casual. Perfect for a visit to a Palm Beach residence, which was definitely in millionaire territory. After all, she did want to assure Cole's mother she was a suitable companion for her in every way.

Her doorbell rang at five minutes to ten. Cole had either given himself more time than he needed to get here, or was keen to get going. Liz grabbed her handbag on the way to the door, intent on presenting herself as ready to leave immediately. She wasn't expecting to have her breathing momentarily paralysed at sight of him, but then she'd never seen him dressed in anything other than an impeccably tailored suit.

Blatant macho virility hit her right in the face. He wore a black polo sweater, black leather jacket, black leather gloves, black jeans, his thick black hair was slightly mussed, adding an air of wild vitality, and his eyes were an electric blue, shooting a bolt of shock straight through Liz's heart.

'Hi!' he said, actually grinning at her. 'You might

need a scarf for your hair. It's a glorious morning so I've put the hood of my car down.'

Scarf...the tiger print scarf for this outfit, she could hear Diana saying. 'Won't be a moment,' she managed to get out and wheeled away, heading for her bedroom to the beat of a suddenly drumming heart, leaving him standing outside her apartment, not even thinking to invite him in. Her mind was stuck on the word, scarf, probably because it served to block out everything else.

Despite the speedy collection of this accessory, Cole had stepped into her living room and was glancing around when she emerged from the bedroom. 'Good space. Nice high ceilings,' he commented appreciatively.

'Built in the nineteen thirties,' she explained on her way to the door, feeling his intrusion too keenly to let him linger in her home.

'Do you own or rent?' he asked curiously.

'It's partly mine. I'm paying off the bank.'

'Fine investment,' he approved.

'I think so. Though primarily I wanted a place of my own.'

'Most women acquire a home through marriage,' he said with a slightly cynical edge.

Or through divorce, Liz thought, wondering how much his almost ex-wife had taken him for and whether that experience had contributed to his detachment from the human race.

'Well, I wasn't counting on that happening,' she said dryly, holding the door and waving him out—a pointed gesture which was ignored.

'You like your independence?' he asked, cocking a quizzical eyebrow at her.

She shrugged. 'Not particularly. I've just found it's better to only count on what I know I can count on.'

'Hard lesson to learn,' he remarked sympathetically.

Had he learnt it, too?

Liz held her tongue. He was finally moving out, waiting for her to lock the door behind them. She didn't know what to think of the probing nature of his conversation. Or was it just casual chat? Maybe she was too used to Cole's habit of never saying anything without purpose.

Still, the sense of being targeted on a personal level persisted and it was some relief that he didn't speak at all as they descended the flight of stairs to street level. Perversely the silence made her more physically aware of him as he walked beside her. She was glad when they emerged into the open air.

It was, indeed, a glorious morning. There was something marvellous about winter sunshine—the warmth and brightness it delivered, the crisp blue of a cloudless sky banishing all thought of cold grey. It lifted one's spirits with its promise of a great day.

'Lucky we don't have to be shut up in the office,' Liz said impulsively, the words accompanied by a smile she couldn't repress.

'An unexpected pleasure,' Cole replied, his smile raising tingles of warmth the sun hadn't yet bestowed.

Liz was piqued into remarking, 'I thought work was the be-all and end-all for you.'

His laser-like eyes actually twinkled at her. 'My life does extend a little further than that.'

Her heart started fluttering. Was he *flirting?* 'Well, obviously, you do care about your mother.'

'Mmmh…a few other things rate my attention, too.'

His slanted look at her caused a skip in her pulse beat and provoked Liz into open confrontation. 'Like what?'

He laughed. He actually laughed. Liz was shocked into staring at him, never having seen or heard Cole Pierson laugh before. It was earth-shaking stuff. He suddenly appeared much younger, happily carefree, and terribly, terribly attractive. The blue eyes danced at her with wicked amusement, causing her to flush in confusion.

'What's so funny?' she demanded.

'Me…you…and here we are.' Still grinning, he gestured to the kerb, redirecting her gaze to the car parked beside it.

Hood down, he'd said, alerting her to the fact that he had to be driving some kind of convertible. If anything, Liz would have assumed a BMW roadster or a Mercedes sports, maybe even a Rolls-Royce Corniche—very expensive, of course, but in a classy conventional style, like his Armani suits.

It was simply impossible to relate the car she was seeing to the boss she knew. She stared at the low-slung, glamorous, silver speed machine in shocked disbelief, her feet rooted on the sidewalk as Cole moved forward and opened the passenger door for her.

'You drive…a Maserati?' Her voice emerged like a half-strangled squawk.

'Uh-huh. The Spyder Cambio Corsa,' he elaborated, naming the model for her.

'A Maserati,' she repeated, looking her astonishment at him.

'Something wrong with it?'

She shook her head, belatedly connecting his current sexy clothes to the sexy car and blurting out, 'This is such a change of image…'

'Welcome to the club,' he said sardonically.

'I beg your pardon?'

She was totally lost with this Cole Pierson, as though he'd changed all the dimensions of his previous persona, emerging as a completely different force to be reckoned with. To top off her sense of everything shifting dangerously between them, he gave her a sizzling head-to-toe appraisal that had her entire skin surface prickling with heat.

'You can hardly deny you've subjected me to a change of image this week, Liz,' he drawled, 'And that was at work, not at play.'

Was he admitting the same kind of disturbance she was feeling now? Whatever…the old boat was being severely rocked on many levels.

'So this is you…at play,' she said in a weak attempt to set things right again.

'One part of me.' There was a challenging glint in his eyes as he waved an invitation to the slinky low black leather passenger seat. 'Shall we go?'

Diana's voice echoed through her head… *Go with the flow.*

Liz forced her feet forward and dropped herself onto the seat as gracefully as she could, swinging her legs in afterwards. 'Thanks,' she murmured as the door was closed for her, then trying for a light note, she smiled and added, 'Nothing like a new experience.'

'You've never ridden in a high-performance car?' he queried as he swung around to the driver's side.

'First time,' she admitted.

'Seems like we're clocking up a few first times between us.'

How many more, Liz thought wildly, acutely aware of him settling in the seat next to her, strong thigh muscles stretching the fabric of his jeans.

'Seat belt,' he reminded her as he fastened his own.

'Right!'

He watched her pull it across her body and click it into place. It made Liz extremely conscious of the belt bisecting her breasts, emphasising their curves.

'Scarf.' Another reminder.

She flushed, quickly spreading the long filmy tiger-print fabric over her hair, winding it around her neck and tying the floating ends at the back.

'Sunglasses.'

It was like a countdown to take-off.

Luckily she always carried sunglasses in her handbag. Having whipped them out and slipped them on, she dared a look at him through the tinted lenses.

He gave her a devil-may-care grin as he slid his own onto his nose. 'You want to watch those jungle prints, Liz. Makes me wonder if you're yearning for a ride on the wild side.'

Without waiting for a reply—which was just as well because she was too flummoxed to think of one—he switched on the engine, put the car into gear, and they were off, the sun in their faces, a wind whipping past, and all sorts of wild things zipping through Liz's mind.

CHAPTER SIX

LIZ couldn't help feeling it was fantastic, riding around in a Maserati. The powerful acceleration of the car meant they could zip into spaces in the traffic that would have closed for less manoeuvrable vehicles. Pedestrians stared enviously at it when they were stopped at traffic lights. They looked at her and Cole, too, probably speculating about who they were, mentally matching them up to the luxurious lifestyle that had to go with such a dream car. After one such stop, Liz was so amused by this she burst out laughing.

'What's tickling your sense of humour?' Cole inquired.

'I feel like the Queen of Sheba and a fraud at the same time,' she answered, grinning at the madness of her being seen as belonging to a Maserati, which couldn't be further than the truth.

'Explain.'

The typical economical command put her on familiar ground again with Cole. 'It's the car,' she answered happily. 'Because I'm your passenger, people are seeing me as someone who has to be special.'

'And you think that's funny?'

'Well, it is, isn't it? I mean you are who you are...but I'm just your employee.'

'Oh, I don't know.' His mouth quirked as he

glanced at her. 'You do have a touch of the Queen of Sheba about you today.'

This comment wasn't boss-like at all. Liz tried to laugh it off but wasn't sure the laughter sounded natural. She was glad he was wearing sunglasses, dimming the expression in the piercing blue eyes. As it was, the soft drawl of his voice had curled around her stomach, making it flutter.

'And why shouldn't they think you're special?' he continued with a longer glance at her. 'I do.'

Liz took a deep breath, desperate to regather her scattered wits. 'That's not the point, Cole. I mean…this car…your wealth…I'm sure you take it all for granted, but it's not me.'

'Do you categorise anyone born to wealth as *special?*' he demanded critically.

'Well…they're at least privileged.'

'Privileged, yes. Which, more times than not, means spoiled, not special.' He shook his head. 'I bought a Maserati because I like high performance. You've remained my P.A. because you give me high performance, too. In my view, you match this car more than any other woman who has ridden in that passenger seat.'

More than the fabulous Tara Summerville?

Liz couldn't believe it.

Unless Cole had acquired the Maserati *after* the separation with his wife.

On second thoughts, he'd been talking performance, not appearance, which reduced the compliment to a work-related thing, puncturing Liz's bubble of pleasure.

'You know, being compared favourably to how well an engine runs doesn't exactly make a woman feel special, Cole,' she dryly informed him.

He laughed. 'So how do I answer you? Hmm...' His brow furrowed in concentration. 'I think you were being a fraud to yourself all the time you were with Brendan, but now you're free of him, the real you has emerged in a blaze of glory and everyone is seeing the shine and recognising how special you are, so you're not a fraud today.' He grinned at her. 'How's that?'

She had to laugh. It was over the top stuff but it did make her feel good, as though she really had shed the miserable cloak of feeling less—deserving less— than her beautiful sisters. 'It wasn't so much Brendan's influence,' she felt obliged to confess. 'I guess I've had a problem with self-esteem for a long time.'

'What on earth for?' he demanded, obviously seeing no cause for it.

She shook her head, not wanting to get into analysing her life. 'Let me relish *blaze of glory*. I can smile over that for the rest of the trip.' Suiting action to words, she gave him her best smile.

He shook his head, still puzzled. 'Would it help for you to know I hold you in the highest esteem?'

'Thank you. It's very kind of you to say so.'

'I can hear a *but* in there.'

Her smile turned rueful. 'I guess what you're giving me is respect for what I can carry out for you. And I'm glad to have your respect. Please don't think I'm not. But I've never felt...incompetent...in that area, Cole. Though I have wondered if being too damned smart is more a curse than a blessing.'

'It's a gift. And it's stupid not to use it. You won't be happy within yourself if you try denying it. You know perfectly well it pleases you to get things right, Liz.'

'Mmmh...but I'm not happy living in a world of my own. I want...' She stopped, realising just how personal this conversation had become, and how embarrassing it might be in retrospect, especially on Monday when she had to face Cole at work again.

'Go on,' he pressed.

She tried shrugging it off. 'Oh, all the usual things a woman wants.'

'Fair enough.'

To Liz's immense relief, he let it go at that. She'd been running off at the mouth, drawn into speaking from her heart instead of her head, all because Cole had somehow invaded her private life and was involving himself in it.

Her gaze drifted to the leather gloved hands on the steering wheel. Power controlling power. A convulsive little shiver of excitement warned her she should get her mind right off tempting fantasies. But it was very difficult with Cole looking as he did, driving this car, and dabbling in highly personal conversation.

She did her best to focus on the passing scenery, a relatively easy task once they hit the road along the northern beaches, passing through Dee Why, Collaroy, Narrabeen, then further on, Bilgola, Avalon, Whale Beach. Apart from the attraction of sand and sea, there were some fabulous homes along the way, making the most of million dollar views. Liz had never actually visited this part of Sydney, knew it only by repute, so it was quite fascinating to see it firsthand.

Finally they came to Palm Beach, right at the end of the peninsula, where large mansions overlooked the ocean on one side and Pittwater the other. Cole turned the Maserati into a semicircular driveway for what looked like a palatial Mediterranean villa with many colonnaded verandahs. It was painted a creamy pink and positively glowed in the sunshine. A fountain of dolphins was centred on the front lawn and a hedge of glorious pink and cream Hawaiian hibiscus lined the driveway.

'Wow!' Liz breathed.

'It is far too large for my mother, requires mountainous maintenance, but she won't leave it,' Cole said in a tone of weary resignation.

'Neither would I,' Liz replied feelingly, turned chiding eyes to Nancy's son. 'She must love it. Leaving would be a terrible wrench.'

Cole sighed. 'She's alone. She's getting old. And she's a long way out from the city.'

Liz understood his point. 'You worry about her.'

He brought the Maserati to a halt, switched off the engine. 'She is my mother,' he stated in the sudden quiet.

And he loved her, thereby passing the functional family background test, unlike Brendan. Liz clamped down on the wayward thought and pushed her mind back onto track.

'I *will* look after her on this trip, Cole.'

He smiled. 'I know I can count on you. And while your ex-boyfriend may not have appreciated your responsible streak, I do. And I don't count on many people for anything.'

Over the past year she had considered him totally self-sufficient. Coldly self-sufficient. It gave Liz a rush of warm pleasure to hear him express some dependence on her, even if it was only peripheral.

No man is an island, she thought.

No woman is, either.

Liz was very conscious of needs that remained unanswered. They'd just been highlighted by Cole's comparing himself to Brendan.

Deliberately highlighted?

For what purpose?

He took off his sunglasses and tucked them into the top pocket of his leather jacket. Liz was prompted into taking hers off, too. She was about to meet his mother again and she didn't need any defensive barrier with Nancy Pierson.

'Want to remove your scarf before we go inside?'

She'd forgotten the scarf, forgotten her hair. Cole sat watching as she quickly unwound the protective cover and tucked it under the collar of her jacket, letting the ends fall loose down the front. Having whipped out a brush from her handbag, she fluffed up her flattened hair and trusted that she hadn't eaten off her lipstick because painting her mouth under Cole's gaze was not on. As it was, she was super conscious of him observing her actions and their effect.

'Okay?' she asked, turning to show herself for his approval.

His eyes weren't their usual ice blue. They seemed to simmer over her face and hair, evoking a flush as he drawled, 'All things bright and beautiful.'

Then he was out of the car and at the passenger door before Liz found the presence of mind to release her seat belt. As she freed herself and swung her feet to the ground, he offered his hand for the long haul upright. It was an automatic response to take it, yet his grip shot an electric charge up her arm and when she rose to her full height, they were standing so close and he seemed so big, she stared at the centre of his throat rather than risk looking up and sparking any realisation of her acute physical awareness of him.

She could even smell the leather, and a hint of male cologne. His broad shoulders dwarfed hers, stirring a sense of sexual vulnerability that quite stunned her because she'd never felt overwhelmed by the close presence of any other man. And this was her boss, who should have been familiar, not striking these weird chords that threatened to change everything between them.

'I didn't realise you were so small,' he murmured in a bemused tone.

Her head jerked up as a sense of belittlement shot through her. The gold sparks in her green eyes blazed at him. 'I hate being *small.*'

His brows drew together in mock concern. 'Correction. Dainty and delicate.'

'Oh, great! Now I sound breakable.'

'Woman of steel?'

His eyes were twinkling.

She took a deep breath and summoned up a wry smile. 'Sorry. You hit a sore point. Unlike you, I was behind the door when God gave out height.'

He openly grinned. 'But you weren't behind the door when God gave out quick wit. Which you'll undoubtedly have to use to keep my mother in line.'

With that comment he led off towards the front door of the pink mansion and Liz fell into step beside him, still fiercely wishing she was as tall as her sisters, which would make her a much better physical match for him. Somehow that 'small' comment felt as though she'd been marked down in the attraction stakes.

On the other hand, she was probably suffering from an overactive imagination to think Cole was attracted at all, and she'd do well to concentrate her mind on exercising the quick wit he credited her with, because the real purpose of this trip was about to get under way.

The front door was opened just as they were stepping up onto the ground floor verandah. 'At last!' Nancy Pierson cried in a tone of pained relief.

Cole checked his watch. 'It's only just eleven, Mum.'

'I know, dear, but I've been counting the minutes since Tara arrived. You could have warned me...'

'Tara?' Cole's face instantly tightened. 'What the devil is she doing here?'

Nancy looked confused. 'She said...'

'You shouldn't have let her in.'

The confusion deepened, hands fluttering a helpless appeal. 'She *is* still your wife.'

'A technicality. One that will end next week.'

This evoked a huff of exasperation from his mother. 'Tara gave me the impression it was arranged for her to meet you here.'

'There's no such arrangement. You've been manipulated, Mum.'

'Well, I'm glad you recognise Tara's skill at doing that, Cole,' came the swift and telling retort. Clearly Nancy held no warm feelings for the woman her son had married. 'I set out morning tea in the conservatory. She's there waiting for you, making herself at home as though she had every right to.'

'Makes for one hell of a scene,' Cole ground out.

'Well, it's not my place to shut her out of your life. It's you who has to make that good. If you have a mind to.'

'Tara's made you doubt it?'

Another huff of exasperation. 'How am I supposed to know what you feel, Cole? You never talk about it. For all I know, you've been pining over that woman...'

'No way!'

'Then you'd better go and convince her of that because she's acting as though she only has to crook her little finger at you and...'

'An act is what it is, Mum.' He flashed a steely glance at Liz. 'As you've just heard, we have some unexpected company for morning tea.'

'I'll take Liz upstairs with me,' Nancy rushed out,

shooting an anguished look at her. 'I'm sorry, dear. This isn't what I planned.'

'Which is precisely why you won't scurry off with Liz,' Cole broke in tersely. 'I will not have her treated like some backroom nonentity because my almost ex-wife decides to barge in on us.'

Nancy looked shocked. 'I didn't mean...'

'It's an issue of discretion, Cole,' Liz quickly supplied. 'I don't mind giving you privacy.'

'Which plays right into Tara's scheme. We're not changing *anything* for her.' Angry pride shifted into icy command. 'Mum, you will lead back to the conservatory. Liz, you will accompany my mother as you normally would. We are going to have the morning tea which has been prepared for *us*.'

He gestured her forward, unshakable determination etched on his face. Liz glanced hesitantly at his mother whom she was supposed to be pleasing today. The anguish was gone from Nancy's expression. In fact, there seemed to be a look of smug delight in her eyes as she, too, waved Liz into the house.

'Please forgive me for not greeting you properly, dear,' she said with an apologetic smile. 'These problems in communication do throw one out.'

'Perfectly understandable,' Liz assured her. Then taking her cue from Cole's command to act normally, she smiled and said, 'I love the look of your home, Nancy. It's very welcoming.'

'How nice of you to say so!' Nancy beamed her pleasure as she hooked her arm around Liz's and drew her into a very spacious foyer, its tiled floor laid out in a fascinating mosaic pattern depicting coral and seashells. 'I picked everything myself for this house. Even these tiles on the floor.'

'They're beautiful,' Liz said in sincere admiration, trying not to be too conscious of Cole closing the door behind them, locking them into a scene that was bound to be fraught with tension and considerable unpleasantness, since Tara Summerville had obviously come expecting to gain something and Cole was intent on denying her.

Nancy continued to point out features of the house as she showed Liz through it, feeding off the interest expressed and enjoying telling little stories about various acquisitions, quite happy not to hurry back to her uninvited guest. Liz suspected Nancy was taking satisfaction in keeping Tara waiting.

Cole didn't push his mother to hurry, either, seemingly content to move at her pace, yet Liz sensed his seething impatience with the situation that had been inflicted on all of them by the woman he'd married.

He must have loved her once, Liz reasoned.

Had the love died, or had husband and wife been pulled apart by grief over the loss of their child?

She had never speculated over her boss's marriage—none of her business—but the exchange between mother and son at the door had ignited a curiosity Liz couldn't deny now. She wanted to see how Cole and Tara Summerville reacted to each other, wanted to know the cause of the ruction between them, wanted to feel Cole was now truly free of his wife...*which may not be the case.*

Surely a private meeting would have served his purpose for ending it more effectively.

Was his angry pride hiding a vulnerability to his wife's power to manipulate his feelings?

Was he using Liz and his mother as a shield, not trusting himself in a one-on-one situation?

As they approached the conservatory, Nancy's prattling began to sound nervous and the tension emanating from Cole seemed to thicken the air, causing Liz to hold her breath. She sensed something bad was about to happen.

Very bad.

And she found herself suddenly wishing she wasn't in the middle of it.

CHAPTER SEVEN

LIZ caught a quick impression of abundant ferns, exotic plants, many pots of gorgeous cyclamens in bloom, all forming a glorious backdrop to settings of cane furniture cushioned in tropical prints. However, even as she entered the conservatory her gaze was drawn to the woman seated at the far end of a long rectangular table.

'Cole, darling…' she drawled, perfect red lips pursing to blow a kiss at him as she rose from her chair, giving them all the full benefit of what the media still termed 'the body' whenever referring to Tara Summerville.

She wore a black leather jacket that moulded every curve underneath it, with enough buttons undone to promise a spillage of lush feminine flesh if one more button was popped. This was teamed with a tight little miniskirt, also in black leather, and with a front split that pointed up the apex of possibly the most photographed legs in history—long, long legs that led down to sexy little ankle high boots. A belt in black and white cowhide was slung jauntily around her hips and a black and white handkerchief scarf was tied at the base of her very long throat.

Her thick mane of tawny hair tumbled down to her shoulder-blades in highly touchable disarray and her artfully made-up amber eyes gleamed a provocative challenge at the man she was intent on targeting. Not so much as a glance at Liz. Nor at Nancy Pierson. This was full power tunnel vision at Cole and Liz suspected the whole beam of it was sizzling with sexual invitation.

'I'm glad you're on your feet, Tara,' Cole said in icy disdain of this approach. 'Just pick up your bag and keep on walking, right out of this house.'

'Very uncivil of you, darling, especially when *your mother* invited me in,' she returned with a cat-like smile, halting by a side chair and gripping the back of it, making a stand against being evicted.

'You lied to her,' came the blunt rebuttal.

'Only to get past your pride, Cole. Now that I'm here for you, why not admit that pride is…' She rolled her hips and moved her mouth into a sensual pout. '…a very cold bedfellow.'

'Waste of time and effort, Tara. Might as well move on. I have,' he stated emphatically.

'Then why haven't I heard a whisper of it?' she mocked, still exuding confidence in her ability to get to him.

'I no longer care to mix in your social circle.'

'You're *news,* Cole. There would have been tattle somewhere if you'd…*moved on.*'

'I prefer to guard my privacy these days.'

He was stonewalling, Liz thought. If there'd been any woman in his life since Tara, some evidence of the relationship would have shown up, at least to her as his personal assistant—telephone calls, bookings to be made, various arrangements. Was it pride, resisting the offer Tara was blatantly making? Or did he truly not want her anymore?

'Don't tell me you've taken to slumming it,' Tara tossed at him derisively.

'Not every woman has your need for the limelight,' Cole returned, icy disdain back in his voice. 'And since I'll never be a party to it again, I strongly recommend you go and find yourself a fellow game player to shine with. You're not about to win anything here.'

Her eyes narrowed, not caring to look defeat in the face. For the first time, her gaze slid to Liz. A quick up and down appraisal left her feeling she'd been raked to the bone. The fact that Nancy was still hugging her arm didn't go unnoticed, either. Without any warning, Tara flashed a bolt of venom at Cole's mother.

'You never did like me, did you, Nancy?'

Liz felt the older woman stiffen under the direct attack, but she was not lacking in firepower herself. 'It's difficult to like such a totally self-centred person as yourself, Tara,' she said with crisp dignity.

A savagely mocking smile was aimed right back at her. 'No doubt you've been producing sweet little protégées for Cole ever since I left.' Her glittering gaze moved to Liz. 'So who and what is this one?'

'*I* brought Liz with me,' Cole stated tersely. 'Her presence here has nothing to do with you and your exit is long overdue.'

'*Your* choice, Cole?' One finely arched eyebrow rose in amused query. 'In place of *me?*'

The comparison was meant to humiliate, but on

seeing his wife in the flesh again, Liz had already conceded she'd never be able to compete in the looks department. She just didn't have the female equipment Tara Summerville had. Not even close to it. But since it could be argued there was something positive to be said for an admirable character and an appealing personality—neither of which was overly evident in Cole's wife—the nasty barb didn't hit too deeply. What actually hurt more was Cole's response to it.

'Oh, for God's sake! Liz has been my personal assistant for the past three years. You used to waltz past her on your way to my office in times gone by, though typically, you probably didn't bother noticing her.'

It was a curt dismissal of the *his choice* tag, implying there was no chance of her ever being anything more than his personal assistant. It shouldn't have felt like a stab to her heart, but it did.

'The little brown mouse!' Tara cried incredulously, then tossed her head back as laughter trilled from her throat.

Liz's stomach knotted. She knew intuitively that Tara Summerville hadn't finished with her. The nerve-jangling laughter was bound to have a nasty point to it. The amber eyes glinted maliciously at her as the remarks rolled.

'How handy, being Cole's P.A.! Saw your chance and took it, jazzing yourself up, making yourself *available,* and here you are, getting your hooks into Mummy, as well, playing Miss All-Round-Perfect.'

The rush of blood to Liz's head was so severe she didn't hear what Cole said, only the angry bark of his voice. She saw the response to it though, Tara swinging back to pick up her bag, slinging the strap of it over her shoulder, strutting towards Cole, pausing to deliver one last broadside.

'You've been *had,* Cole. No doubt she's hitting all the right chords for you…but I bet she can't match me in bed. Think about it, darling. It's not too late to change your mind.'

Both of them left the conservatory, Tara leading off like a victor who'd done maximum damage, Cole squeezing Liz's shoulder first in a silent gesture of appreciation for her forebearance, then following Tara out to enforce her departure and possibly have the last word before she left.

Liz was so sick with embarrassment, she didn't know what to do or say. The worst of it was, Tara had literally been echoing Diana's calculated plan to *get the boss*. While that had not been part of Liz's motivation for going along with her sisters' makeover plan, Tara's accusations had her squirming with guilt over the feelings that had emerged this past week, the growing desire for Cole to find her attractive.

Fortunately, Nancy moved straight into hostess mode, drawing Liz over to the table and filling the awkward silence with a torrent of words. 'Tara always did make an ugly scene when she wasn't getting her own way. You mustn't take anything she said to heart, dear. Pure spite. You just sit yourself down and relax and I'll make us a fresh pot of tea. Help yourself to a pastry or a scone with strawberry jam and cream. That's Cole's favourite. I always make him Devonshire tea.'

Liz sat. Her gaze skated distractedly over a selection of small Danish pastries with fillings of glazed fruit—apricot, apple, peach—the plate of scones beside dishes of cream and strawberry jam. Nothing prompted an appetite. She thought she would choke on food.

Nancy moved to what was obviously a drinks bar, easily accessible to the swimming pool beyond the conservatory. She busied herself behind it, apparently unaffected by the suggestion that Liz and Cole were having an affair, though she must be suspecting it now, adding in the fact that Cole had arranged for his P.A. to accompany her on a pleasure trip. It was, after all, an extraordinary thing to do, given there was no closer connection between them than boss and employee.

Liz couldn't bear Nancy thinking she was Cole's mistress on the side. It made her seem underhand, sleazy, hiding the intimacy from his mother, pretending everything was straight and aboveboard.

'I'm not having a secret affair with Cole. I've never slept with him…or…or anything like that,' she blurted out, compelled to clear any murkiness from their relationship.

Nancy looked up from her tea-making, startled by the emphatic claim. Her blue eyes were very direct, projecting absolute certainty as she replied, 'I have no doubt whatsoever about that, dear. I questioned Cole about you before we met on Monday. His answers revealed…' She heaved a deep sigh. '…he only thought of you as very capable.'

The flush in Liz's cheeks still burned. Although she'd known Cole had not been aware of her as a woman, certainly not before this past week, that truth was not quite so absolute now. He *was* seeing her differently, and even though it might not *mean* what Diana wanted it to mean, Liz couldn't let Tara's interpretation of her changed appearance go unanswered.

'I'm not out to *get* him, either.'

Nancy heaved another deep sigh, then gave her a sad little smile. 'I almost wish you were, dear, but I don't think it's in your nature.'

It startled Liz out of her wretched angst. 'You wish…?'

'I probably shouldn't say this…' Nancy's grimace revealed her own inner angst. '…but I'm very afraid Cole is still stuck on Tara. What she said is all too true. And I'm sure you must know it, as well. There hasn't been any other woman in his life since she left him. It's like he's sealed himself off from every normal social connection.'

Liz nodded. She was well acquainted with *the untouchable ice man*.

Nancy rattled on, voicing her main concern. 'But if Tara is now determined on getting her hooks into him again…' A shake of the head. 'I can only hope Cole has the good sense to go through with the divorce and have done with her.'

Liz kept her mouth shut. It wasn't appropriate for her to comment on Cole's personal life when it had nothing to do with her. The stress of Tara's visit had wrung this confidence from Nancy, just as it had driven Liz to defend herself. Where the truth lay about Cole's feelings for his wife, she had no idea.

Though now that Nancy had spelled out her viewpoint, it did seem he had to be carrying a lot of emotional baggage from his marriage—baggage he'd systematically buried under intensive work.

Was the physical confrontation with his wife stirring it all up? He hadn't come back from seeing her out of the house. Maybe they were still talking, arguing as couples do when neither of them really wanted to let go. Any foothold—even a bitter one— was better than none. And Cole was unhampered by witnesses now. What if Tara had thrown her arms around him, physically pressing for a resumption of intimacy? Was it possible for him to be totally immune to what 'the body' was offering?

A sick depression rolled through Liz. Cole had only noticed her this past week because *the little brown mouse* didn't fit that label anymore. Which was probably still an annoyance to him. Or a curiosity, given his questioning about Brendan. Nothing to do with a sudden attraction which she'd probably fabricated out of her own secret wanting it to be so.

A foolish fantasy.

Why on earth would a man like him—a handsome billionaire—be attracted to her when he could snap his fingers and have the Tara Summervilles of this world? She must have been mad to let Diana influence her thinking. Or desperate to feel something excitingly positive after being dumped by Brendan.

'Oh! There's Cole with the tradesman!' Nancy cried in relief.

The remark halted Liz's miserable reverie and directed her gaze out to the pool area where Nancy was looking. Cole was, indeed, with another man, pointing out a section of paving and leading him towards it.

'He must have arrived while Cole was seeing Tara out. They've come down the side path,' Nancy prattled on, her spirits perking up at this evidence that her son's delayed return did not mean he was being vamped by his almost ex-wife. 'The appointment was at eleven o'clock, after all. So fortuitous.'

It didn't guarantee that Cole had maintained his rejection of any reunion, but it certainly minimised the opportunity for persuasion on his wife's part. Liz found herself hoping that Tara had not *won* anything from him, and not just because of being interrupted by the arrival of the tradesman. Nancy didn't like the woman and Liz certainly had no reason to. But no doubt the power of sex could turn some men blind to everything else.

'Now we can enjoy our morning tea,' Nancy declared, carrying an elegant china teapot to the table and setting it down with an air of happy satisfaction. Clearly danger had been averted in her mind. She settled on the chair opposite to Liz's and eyed her with bright curiosity.

'Pardon me for asking, dear, but was it just this week that you…uh…jazzed yourself up?'

'During my vacation,' Liz answered, not minding the question from Nancy, knowing she could find out from Cole anyway. 'My sisters ganged up on me, saying I'd let myself become drab, and hauled me off to do their Cinderella trick.'

'Well, whatever they did, you do look lovely.'

'Thank you.'

'Tea?'

'Yes, please.'

Nancy poured. 'So you came back to work on Monday with a new image,' she said, smiling encouragement.

'Yes.'

'Did Cole notice any difference?'

Liz grimaced. 'He didn't like it.'

'Didn't like how you looked?'

'Didn't like me looking different, I think.' Liz shrugged. 'No doubt he'll get used to it.'

'Milk and sugar?'

Liz shook her head. 'Just as it is, thank you.'

'Do have a scone, dear.'

Liz took one out of politeness, though she did feel calmer now and thought there'd be no problem with swallowing. It was a relief to have Nancy understanding her situation. It would have been extremely uncomfortable accompanying Cole's mother on the trip, with her still thinking all sorts of horribly false things.

Having cut the scone in half, Liz was conscientiously spooning strawberry jam and cream onto her plate when her ragged nerves received another jolt.

'Oh, good! Cole is coming in for his tea,' Nancy announced, causing Liz to jerk around in her chair to see her boss skirting the pool and heading for the conservatory, having left the tradesman to measure the paving area and calculate the cost of the work to be done.

Totally mortified by the tide of heat that rushed up her neck again, Liz focused hard on transferring the jam and cream to the halved scone. If she shoved the food into her mouth and appeared to be eating, she reasoned that Cole might only speak to his mother. It might be a cowardly tactic but she didn't feel up to coping with his penetrating gaze and probing questions. She didn't even want to look at him. He might have lipstick smudged on his mouth.

Which was none of her business!

Why she felt so violent about that she didn't know and didn't want to know. She just wanted to be left out of anything to do with Tara Summerville.

She heard a glass door slide open behind her and it felt as though a whoosh of electric energy suddenly permeated the air. Her hands started trembling. It stopped her from lifting the scone to her mouth. She glared at her plate, hating being affected like this. It wasn't fair. She'd done nothing wrong.

'Liz...'

She gritted her teeth.

He had no right to put her on the spot, commanding her attention when they weren't even at work. She was here in her spare time, as a favour to his mother, not as *his* personal assistant.

'Are you okay?' he asked, amazingly in a tone of concern.

Pride whipped her head around to face him. There was no trace of red lipstick on his mouth. His expression was one of taut determination, the piercing blue eyes intensely concentrated, aimed at searching her mind for any trouble.

Her chin tilted in direct challenge as she stated, 'I have no reason not to be okay.'

He gave a slow nod. 'I didn't anticipate a collateral hit from Tara. I regret you were subjected to it.'

'A hit only works if there's damage done. I've assured your mother there's no truth in what was assumed about me…and you.' *And don't you dare think otherwise,* she fiercely telegraphed to him.

His gaze flicked sharply to Nancy. 'You didn't believe that rank bitchiness, did you, Mum?'

'No, dear. And I told Liz so.'

'Right! No harm done then,' he said, apparently satisfied. 'Got to get back to check that this guy knows what's he's quoting on.'

'What about your tea?' Nancy asked.

'I'll have it later.'

He stepped outside, closed the door, and to all intents and purposes, the nasty incident with Tara Summerville was also closed. Liz certainly wasn't about to bring the subject up again. She realised her hands were clenched in her lap and consciously relaxed them. The scone was waiting to be eaten. She'd eat it if it killed her. It proved she was okay.

'Well, isn't that nice?' Nancy remarked, beaming pleasure at her as Liz lifted one half of the scone from her plate.

She looked blankly at Cole's mother, completely lost on whatever had struck her as *nice.*

'He cares about you, dear.' This said with a benevolent smile that thoroughly approved of the supposed caring.

Liz felt too frazzled to argue the point.

She only hoped that Cole had completely dismissed the idea—planted by Tara—that his personal assistant was focused far more on climbing into bed with him than doing the work she was employed to do.

CHAPTER EIGHT

MAKE another baby...

Cole seethed over Tara's last toss at him and all the memories it aroused. He ended up accepting the quotation for the paving work around the pool without even questioning it. He didn't care if the guy was overcharging. As long as the job was done by a reputable tradesman, the cost was irrelevant. All the money in the world could not buy back the life of the baby son he'd lost. Though it could obviously buy back a wife who was prepared to pay lip-service to being a mother again.

A mother...

What a black joke that was!

And the gross insensitivity of Tara's even thinking he'd consider her proposition was typical of her total lack of empathy to how he felt. God! He wouldn't want her in the same house as any child of his, let alone being the biological mother to it, having the power to affect its upbringing in so many negative ways.

David had only ever been a show-off baby to her—trotting him out in designer clothes when it suited her, ignoring him when he needed her. *Their son* hadn't even left a hole in her life when he died, and she'd resented the huge hole he'd left in Cole's—impatient with his grief, ranting about how cold he was to her, seeking more cheerful company because he was such *a drag*.

Did Tara imagine he could forget all that just because they'd started out having great sex and she still had 'the body' to excite him again if she put her mind to it?

He hadn't even felt a tingle in his groin when she'd tried her come-on this morning.

Not a tingle.

Though he had felt a blaze of fury when she'd painted Liz in her own manipulative colours, casting her as a calculating seductress, mocking her efforts to look more attractive. Which she certainly did, though Cole had no doubt the change had been motivated by a need to lift herself out of the doldrums caused by Brendan's defection. Nothing to do with him.

If Liz withered back into a little brown mouse now...because of Tara's bitchiness...Cole seethed over that, too, as he made his way back to the conservatory after seeing the tradesman off. Liz had insisted she was okay, but she hadn't wanted to look at him when he'd asked. When she had turned to answer, her eyes had been all glittery, her cheeks red hot. She'd denied any damage done but Cole suspected her newly grown confidence in herself as a woman had been badly undermined. He wanted to fix that but how...?

Liz and his mother were gone from the conservatory by the time he returned to it, Just as well, since he had no ready antidote for Tara's poison. At least he could trust his mother to be kind to Liz, involve her in the business of packing for their trip. Probably overkind, trying to make up for the nasty taste left behind by her uninvited guest.

He'd made one hell of a mistake marrying that woman. Five more days and the divorce would become final. Thursday. It couldn't come fast enough for Cole.

He made himself a fresh pot of tea, wolfed down a couple of scones, found the morning newspaper and concentrated on shutting Tara out of his mind. She didn't deserve space in it and he wouldn't give it to her.

Having read everything he deemed worth reading, he was attacking the cryptic crossword when his mother returned to the conservatory, wheeling a traymobile loaded with lunch things. Liz trailed behind her, looking anywhere but at him.

'Well, we've worked everything out for the trip,' his mother declared with satisfaction. 'Do clear the table of that newspaper, Cole. And if you'd open a good bottle of red—Cabernet Sauvignon?'

'What are we eating?' he asked, hoping some mundane conversation would make Liz feel more relaxed in his company.

'Lasagne and salad and crispy bread, followed by caramelised pears. And we must hurry because Liz needs to do some shopping and it's after one o'clock already.'

'How much shopping?' he asked as he moved to the bar. 'Mum, have you been pressing Liz to buy a whole lot of stuff to fit what *you* think is needed?'

'Only a few things,' she answered airily. 'Liz didn't understand about the colonial night at The

Strand Hotel in Rangoon where the ladies are invited to wear white, and…'

'Surely it's not obligatory.'

'That's not the point, dear. It's the spirit of the thing.'

He frowned, wondering how much expense his mother was notching up for her companion—costs he simply hadn't envisaged. 'I didn't mean for Liz to be out of pocket over this trip.'

His mother gave him one of those limpidly innocent smiles that spelled trouble. 'Then you could take her shopping so she'll feel right…everywhere we go together.'

'No!' Liz looked horrified by the suggestion, stopping in her setting of cutlery on the table to make a firm stand on the issue. 'You're giving me the trip free, Cole,' she reminded him with vigour. 'And Nancy, I'll get plenty of use out of what I buy anyway. It's no problem.'

The line was drawn and her eyes fiercely defied either of them to cross it.

Cole felt the line all through lunch.

He was her boss.

She was here on assignment.

She would oblige his mother in every way in regard to the trip, but the block on any personal rapport with the man who employed her was rigidly adhered to. She barely looked at him and avoided acknowledging his presence as much as she could without being openly rude. It was very clear to him that what Tara had said about her—and him—was preying on Liz's mind.

It was even worse in the car travelling back into the city. She sat almost scrunched up in the passenger seat, making herself as small as possible, her hands tightly interlinked in her lap. No joy in riding in the Maserati this time, though Cole sensed she was willing the car to go as fast as it could, wanting the trip over and done with so she could get away from him.

It made him angry.

He hated Tara's power to do this to her.

Just because Liz wasn't built like Tara didn't make her less attractive in her own individual way. He liked the new hairstyle on her. It was perky. Drew more attention to her face, too, which had a bright vitality that was very appealing. Very watchable. Particularly her eyes. A lot of power in those sparkly green eyes. As for her figure, certainly on the petite side, but definitely feminine. Sexy, too, in the clothes she'd been wearing. Not in your face sexy. More subtle. Though strong enough to get to him this past week.

Cole was tempted to say so, but he wasn't sure she'd want to hear such things from him, coming on top of Tara's coupling them as she had. It might make Liz shrink even more inside herself, thinking he *was* about to make a move on her. It was damned difficult, given their work situation and her current fragile state.

'I'd appreciate it if you'll drop me off along Military Road at the Mosman shopping centre,' she said abruptly.

He glanced at his watch. Almost three o'clock. Most shops closed at five o'clock on Saturday, except in tourist areas, and Mosman was more a classy suburb. 'I'll park and wait for you. Take you home when you're through shopping.'

'No, please.' Almost a panicky note in her voice. 'I don't want to hold you up.'

'*You'll* be held up, getting public transport home. Apart from which, you wouldn't be shopping but for my mother making you feel you have to,' he argued. 'I'll sit over coffee somewhere and wait for you.'

'I truly don't want you to do that, Cole.' Very tense. 'It will make me feel I have to hurry.'

'Take all the time you want,' he tossed back at her, assuming a totally relaxed air. 'I have nothing in particular to go home to.'

And he didn't like the sense of her running away from him.

A compelling urge to smash the line she had drawn prompted him into adding, 'Actually, I think I'll tag along with you. Give an opinion on what looks good.'

That shocked her out of her defensive shell. Her head jerked towards him. The sunglasses hid the expression in her eyes but if it was horror, he didn't care.

'I will not let you buy anything for me,' she threw at him, a feisty pride rising out of the assault on her grimly held sense of propriety. 'You are not responsible for…for…'

'My mother's love of dressing up for an occasion?' he finished for her, grinning at the steam he'd stoked. 'I couldn't agree more. The responsibility is all yours for indulging her. And you probably don't need me along. Have to admit the clothes you've been wearing this past week demonstrate you have a great eye for what looks good on you.'

Got in that little boost to her confidence, Cole thought, and continued on his roll with a sense of triumphant satisfaction. 'But most women like a man's opinion and since I'm here on the spot, why not? More interesting for me than sitting over coffee by myself.'

'Cole, I'm your P.A., not your…your…'

Lover? Mistress? Wife?

Clearly she couldn't bring herself to voice such provocative positions. Cole relieved her agitation by putting their relationship back on terms she was comfortable with.

'As your boss, who instigated this whole situation, it's clearly within my authority to see that you don't spend too much on pleasing my mother.'

'I'm not stupid!' she cried in exasperation. 'I said I'd only buy what I'll make use of again.'

'Then you can't have any objection to my feeling right about this. Besides, I'll be handy. I'll carry your shopping bags.'

She shook her head in a helpless fashion and slumped back into silence. Cole sensed that resistance was still simmering but he was now determined on this course of action and he was not about to budge from it. Tara was not going to win over Liz Hart. One way or another, he was going to make Liz feel great about herself.

As she should.

She was great at everything she did for him.

Probably make a great mother, too.

Cole grimaced over this last thought.

Time he got Tara out of his head, once and for all. She'd left one hell of a lot of scar tissue but that was no reason for him not to move on. In fact, he'd told her he had, which had spurred the attack on Liz.

Well, at least he was moving on neutralising that—one step in the right direction.

CHAPTER NINE

LIZ'S heart was galloping. Why, why, why was Cole being so perverse, insisting on going shopping with her, foiling her bid to escape the awkwardness she now felt with him? Didn't he realise how personal it was, giving his opinion on what clothes she chose, carrying her shopping bags, acting as though they were *a couple?*

She took several deep breaths in an attempt to calm herself down. Her mind frantically re-examined everything he'd said, searching for clues that might help her understand his motivation. It came as some relief to realise he couldn't think she'd been making a play for him this past week. His comment on the clothes she'd worn to work had been a compliment on her taste, no hint of suspicion that they could have been especially aimed to attract *his* notice.

He'd said he had nothing in particular to go home to and tagging along with her would be more interesting than drinking coffee alone. But weren't men bored by clothes shopping? Brendan had always been impatient with any time spent on it. *That'll do,* had been his usual comment, never a considered opinion on how good anything looked on her.

Maybe with having a famous model as his wife, Cole had learnt some of the tricks of the trade, but thinking of Tara made Liz even more self-conscious about parading clothes in front of him. She couldn't compete. She didn't want to compete. She just wanted to be left alone to lick her wounds in private.

But Cole was already parking the car, pressing the mechanism that installed the hood, getting ready to leave the Maserati in the street while he accompanied her. She knew there'd be no stopping him. Once Cole Pierson made up his mind to do something, no force on earth would deter him from pursuing his goal. But what was his goal here?

Was it just filling in time with her?

She could minimise the shopping as much as seemed reasonable to him.

Reasonable might be the key. He'd said he wanted to *feel right* about what she bought. Which linked this whole thing back to indulging his mother. Nothing really personal at all.

The frenzy in her mind abated. She could cope with this. She had to. Cole was now out of the car and striding around it to the passenger door. Liz hastily released her safety belt and grabbed her handbag from the floor. The door was opened and once again he offered his hand to help her out. Ignoring it was impossible. Liz took it and was instantly swamped by a wave of dynamic energy that fuzzed the coping sector in her mind.

Thankfully he didn't hold on to her hand, releasing it to wave up and down the street, good-naturedly asking, 'Which way do you want to go?'

Liz paused a moment to orient herself. They were in the middle of the shopping centre. Mosman had quite a number of classy boutiques, but her current budget wasn't up to paying their prices, not after the big splurge she'd just had on clothes. She hadn't wanted to ask Diana for help with these extras for the trip. Her sister would inevitably pepper her with questions about her boss, and Liz didn't want to hear them, let alone answer them. There was, however, one inexpensive shop here that might provide all she needed.

'Across the road and to our left,' she directed.

Cole automatically took her arm to steer her safely through the cruising traffic to the opposite sidewalk. She knew it was a courtesy but it felt like a physical claim on her. She was becoming far, far too conscious of her boss as a man. It wasn't even a relief when he resumed simply walking side by side.

'Do you have a particular place in mind?' he asked, glancing at display windows they passed.

'Yes. It's just along here.' She kept her gaze forward, refusing to be tempted by what she couldn't afford. It was the middle of winter but the new spring fashions were already on show everywhere.

'Hold it!' Cole grabbed her arm to halt her progress and pointed to a mannequin dressed in a gorgeous green pantsuit. 'That would be fantastic on you, Liz.'

'Not what I'm looking for,' she swiftly stated, knowing the classy outfit would cost mega-dollars.

He frowned at her as she tugged herself loose and kept walking. 'What are you looking for?'

'A couple of evening tops to go with black slacks and something in white,' she rattled out.

'Black,' he repeated in a tone of disapproval.

'You're going into the tropics, you know. Hot and humid. You should be wearing something light.'

'Black goes anywhere,' she argued.

'I like green on you,' he argued back.

'What you like isn't really relevant, Cole. You won't be there,' she reminded him, glad to make the point that she wasn't out to please *him*.

'My mother would like what I like,' he declared authoritatively. 'I think we should go back and…'

'No. I'm going to look in here,' she insisted, heading into the shop she had targeted.

It was somewhat overcrowded with racks of clothes, but promising a large range of choice which was bound to yield something suitable. However, Liz had barely reached the first rack when Cole grabbed her hand and hauled her outside.

'A second-hand shop?' he hissed, his black brows beetling down at her.

'Quite a lot of second-hand designer wear,' she tersely informed him. 'Classy clothes that have only been worn a few times, if that. They're great bargains and perfectly good.'

'I will not have you wearing some other woman's cast-offs,' he said so vehemently Liz was stunned into silence, not understanding why he found it offensive. His hand lifted and cupped her cheek, his thumb tilting her chin up so the piercing blue eyes bored into hers with commanding intensity. 'I will not have you thinking you only rate seconds. You're a class act, Liz Hart. Top of the top. And you are going to be dressed accordingly.'

He dropped his hand, hooked her arm around his

and marched her back down the street before Liz could find her voice. Her cheek was still burning from his touch and her heartbeat was thundering in her ears. It was difficult to think coherently with his body brushing hers, his long stride forcing her to pick up pace to keep level with him. Nevertheless, something had to be said.

'Cole, I've…I've spent most of my spare money on…on…'

'I'll do the buying,' he cut in decisively. 'Consider it a bonus for being the best P.A. I've ever had.'

Bonus…best P.A.…top of the top…the heady words buzzed around her brain. The compliments were so extraordinary, exhilarating. And suddenly she recalled what his mother had said—*He cares about you.*

Her feet were almost dancing as he swept her into the boutique she had bypassed before. 'We'll try that green,' he told the saleswoman, pointing to the pantsuit on the display mannequin.

There was such a strong flow of power emanating from Cole, the woman virtually jumped to obey. Liz was ushered into a dressing-room and handed the garments in her size in double-quick time.

'I want to see that on,' Cole continued in commanding vein. 'And while Liz is changing, you can show me anything else you have that might do her justice.'

Wearing second-hand clothes had never bothered her, but Cole's determination to *do her justice* was too intoxicating to resist. She fell in love with the apple green pantsuit and his raking look of male appreciation and resounding, 'Yes,' set her heart fluttering with wild excitement. He really did see her as special...and attractive.

Next came a lime green cotton knit top, sleeveless but with a deep cowl neckline that could be positioned many clever ways. It was teamed with white pants printed with lime green pears, strawberries and mangos—the kind of fun item she'd never indulged in. But it did look brilliant on her and she was tempted into striking a jaunty pose when showing the outfit to Cole. He grinned at her, giving a thumbs up sign, and she grinned back, enjoying the madness of the moment. Both green tops would dress up her black slacks, she decided, trying to be a bit sensible.

'That's it for here,' he declared. 'We'll try somewhere else for the white.'

Somewhere else turned out to be a Carla Zampatti boutique, all stocked up with the new spring range from one of the top designers in Australia. With the help of the saleswoman Cole selected a white broderie anglaise skirt with a ruffle hem and a matching peasant blouse. The correct accessories included a dark auburn raffia hip belt featuring a large red, brown and camel stone clip fastening, long Indian earrings dangling with beads and feathers in the same colours, high wedge heeled sandals in white, with straps that crisscrossed halfway up Liz's calves.

The whole effect was absolutely stunning.

Liz couldn't believe how good she looked.

Fine feathers certainly did make fine birds, she thought giddily, waltzing out of the dressing-room on cloud nine. Cole's gaze fastened on her ankles and slowly travelled up, lingering on her bare shoulder where the saleswoman had pulled down the peasant neckline for *the right effect.* A sensual little smile was directed at the exotic earrings and when he finally met her eyes, she saw the simmer of sexual interest in his—unmistakable—and felt her toes curling in response.

'This strappy bandeau top in camel jersey also goes with that skirt,' the saleswoman informed, showing the garment.

'Yes,' Cole said eagerly. 'Let's see it on.'

It fit very snugly, moulding her small firm breasts, which didn't go unnoticed by Cole whose interest in dressing her as *he* liked seemed to gather more momentum. 'I like that filmy leopard print top, too,' he said, pointing to a rack of clothes.

'The silk georgette with the hanky hemmed sleeve?' It was held up for his approval.

'Mmmh...very sexy.'

'It teams well with the bronze satin pants, and the bronze tassel belt,' the saleswoman encouraged, seizing advantage of the obvious fact that Cole was in a buying mood.

Liz felt driven to protest. 'I don't need any more. Truly.'

'Just this one extra lot then,' came the blithe reply. He grinned at her. 'I know you've got bronze shoes. Saw you wearing them last week. And the jungle motif is definitely your style.'

He would not be deterred. Liz couldn't help feeling both elated and guilty as they left the boutique, both of them now laden with shopping bags.

'Happy?' he asked, triumph sparkling in his eyes.

'Yes. But I shouldn't have let you do that.'

He arched a cocky eyebrow at her. 'The choice was all mine.'

She heaved a sigh in the hope of relieving the wild drumming in her chest. 'You've been very generous. Thank you.'

He laughed. 'It was fun, Liz. Maybe that's what both of us need right now. Some fun.'

His eyes flirted with hers.

It was happening. It really was happening. Just as Diana had predicted. But could a classy appearance achieve so much difference in how one was viewed? It didn't seem right. Surely attraction shouldn't depend entirely on surface image. Yet Cole had *married* Tara Summerville, which pointed to his being heavily swayed by how a woman looked.

But he knows me, the person, too, Liz quickly argued to herself. We've worked together for three years. *Best P.A. I've ever had.* And he did like her. Trust and respect were also mixed in with the liking. So this suddenly strong feeling of attraction was acceptable, wasn't it? Not just a fleeting thing of the moment?

They reached the Maserati and Cole unlocked the boot to stow away the host of shopping bags. 'What we should do now…' he said as they unloaded themselves. '…is drop this stuff off at your apartment, then go out to dinner to celebrate.'

'Celebrate what? Your outrageous extravagance?'

'Worth every cent.' He shut the lid of the boot with an air of satisfaction, then smiled at her. 'Pleasure can't always be so easily bought, Liz, and here we are, both of us riding a high.'

She couldn't deny it, but she knew her high was fired by feelings that hadn't been stirred for a very long time, feelings that had nothing to do with new clothes. Not even fabulous clothes. 'So we're celebrating pleasure?'

'Why not?' He took her arm to steer her to the passenger side, opening the door for her as he added, 'Let's put the blight of our ex-partners aside for one night and focus on having fun.'

One night…

The limitation was sobering. So was the reference to ex-partners. As Liz stepped into the car and settled on the passenger seat, she forced herself to take stock of what these remarks could mean. She herself had completely forgotten the blight left by Brendan in the excitement of feeling the sizzle of mutual attraction with Cole. However, she did have three weeks' distance since last being with Brendan. Cole had been very freshly reminded of his relationship with Tara this morning.

Earlier, before the shopping spree, he'd said he had nothing to go home to. Tara had clearly left a huge hole in his life. Had he just been buying a filler for that hole? As well as some sweet private revenge on the woman who'd taken him for much more than Liz would ever cost him?

She glanced sharply at him as he took the driver's seat beside her. One night of fun could mess with their business relationship. Had Cole thought of that or was he in the mood not to care?

He switched on the engine and threw her a smile that quickened her pulse-beat again. 'How about Doyle's at Rose Bay? Feel like feasting on oysters and lobster?'

Oh, why not? she thought recklessly. There was nothing for her to go home to, either. 'Sounds good. But it's Saturday night. Will we get a table?' The famous seafood restaurant on Sydney Harbour was very popular.

'No problem,' he confidently assured her. 'I'll call and book from your apartment.'

No doubt he wouldn't care what it cost for the restaurant to *find* an extra table for two. Cole was on a roll, intent on sweeping her along with him, and Liz decided not to worry about it. Fun was the order of the night and there was nothing wrong with taking pleasure in each other's company.

Diana's advice slid into her mind.

Go with the flow.

For too much of her life Liz had been managing situations, balancing pros and cons, thinking through all the possible factors, choosing what seemed the most beneficial course. She wanted to be free of all that…if only for one night…to simply *go with the flow* and let Cole take care of whatever happened between them.

After all, he was the boss.

The man in command.

CHAPTER TEN

COLE had never thought of his P.A. as delightful, but she was. Maybe it was the influence of the champagne, loosening inhibitions, bringing out bubbles in her personality. It was the first time she'd ever drunk alcohol in his presence. First time they'd ever been away from their work situation, dining together as a social twosome. She was enjoying the fine dinner at Doyle's and he was thoroughly enjoying her company.

Aware that she liked travelling, he'd prompted her into relating what trips she'd like to take in future—the old silk route from Beijing to Moscow, the northwest passage to Alaska, the Inca trail in South America—places he'd never thought of going himself. He'd hit all the high spots—New York, London, Paris, Milan, Hong Kong—but they hadn't been adventures in the sense Liz was talking about—reliving history and relating culture to geography.

Watching her face light up with enthusiasm, her eyes sparkle in anticipation of all there was yet to see and know, Cole mentally kicked himself for allowing his world to become so narrow, so concentrated on the challenge of accumulating more and more money. He should take more time out, make a few journeys into other areas. Though he'd probably need Liz to guide him into seeing what she saw.

Future plans…he had none. Not really. Just keep on doing what he'd been doing. He looked at Liz, taking pleasure in her vitality, in her quest for new experiences, and a question popped into his mind—a question he asked without any forethought of what its impact might be on her.

'Does marriage and having a family fit anywhere in your future, Liz?'

A shadow instantly descended, wiping the sparkle from her eyes, robbing her face of all expression. Her lashes lowered to half mast, as though marking the death of her hopes in that area, and Cole mentally kicked himself for bringing up what must be a raw subject for her with Brendan having walked away from their long-term relationship.

Her shoulders squared. An ironic little smile tilted one corner of her mouth. Her eyes flashed bleakly at him. 'I guess I'm a failure at being desirable wife material. I haven't met anyone who wants to marry me,' she said in a tone of flat defeat.

Cole barely bit down on the urge to tell her she was intensely desirable in every way. Words were useless if they didn't match her experience. But they were true nonetheless. It had been growing on him all day…how different she was to Tara, how much he liked her, how sexy she looked in the right clothes.

His gaze fastened on her mouth. He wanted to kiss away the hurt that had just been spoken, make her smile with joy again, as she had this afternoon, twirling around in that very fetching white skirt. She'd felt all woman then, failing in nothing, and certainly stirring a few pressing male fantasies in Cole.

'What about you?' she asked. 'Would you come at marriage again?'

It jolted him into a harsh little laugh. 'Not in a hurry.'

'Bad experience?'

'Bad judgment on my part.' He shrugged, not wanting to talk about it. 'Though I would like to be a father again,' he added, admitting that joy and sorrow from his marriage.

She nodded, her eyes flashing heartfelt sympathy. 'I would hate to lose a child of mine.'

It had barely caused a ripple in Tara's life, which made her proposition today all the more obscene. He had no doubt Liz would manage motherhood better, probably dote on a child of her own. He recalled her speaking of a number of sisters to his mother and asked about her family, moving the conversation on.

She was an aunt to two nieces and nephews, had a big extended family, lots of affection in her voice. Good people, Cole thought, and wondered how much he'd missed by being an only child. His father hadn't wanted more, even one being an intrusion on the orderly life he'd liked. Though he had been proud of Cole's achievements.

His mother would have liked a daughter. Someone like Liz with whom she could really share things. Not like Tara.

Liz Hart...

Why hadn't he thought of her like this before?

Blind to what was under his nose.

Tara getting in the way, skewing his view, killing

any desire to even look at a woman, let alone involve himself with one.

Besides which, Liz had been attached—might still be emotionally attached—to the guy who'd used her for years, then dumped her. Though clearly she'd been trying to rise out of those ashes, firing herself up to make something else of her life. Still, she'd definitely been burned, thinking of herself as a failure in the female stakes.

It wasn't right.

And on top of that, Tara putting her down this morning.

So wrong.

The rank injustice that had been done to Liz lingered in Cole's mind, even as he drove her home from Doyle's. She was quiet, the bubbles of the night having fizzed out. Facing the prospect of a lonely apartment, he thought, and memories that would bring misery. He didn't like this thought. He didn't like it one bit.

It was just a one off night, Liz told herself, trying to drum it into her foolish head. And she'd probably talked far too much about herself, her tongue let loose by the free flow of beautiful French champagne, delicious food, and Cole showing so much personal interest in her.

But it hadn't been a two way street. Very little had come back to her about him, and on the question of marriage, Cole's instant and derisive reply—*Not in a hurry*—had burst Liz's fantasy bubble. In fact, reflecting on his manner to her over dinner, Liz decided he undoubtedly dealt with clients in the same fashion, drawing them out, listening intently, lots of eye contact, projecting interest. *Charm,* Jayne had called it.

It didn't *mean* anything.

He'd spelled it out beforehand—one night of fun. And now he was driving her home. Nothing more was going to happen. She just wished her nerves would stop leaping around and she'd be able to make the parting smooth and graceful, showing she didn't expect any more from him.

But in her heart she wanted more.

And trying to argue it away wasn't working. The wanting had been building all day. It was now a heaviness in her chest that was impossible to dislodge. A tight heaviness that was loaded down with sadness, as well. Crying for the moon, she thought. Which had shone on her for a little while this evening but would inevitably keep moving and leave her in the dark again.

Cole parked the car outside her apartment, switched off the headlights. Liz felt enveloped in darkness—a lonely darkness, bereft of the vital power of his presence as he left her to stride around to the passenger side. *Get used to it, girl,* she told herself savagely. *He's not for you.*

The door opened and she stepped out, not taking the offered hand this time, forcing herself upright on her own two legs because if she took that hand it would heat hers, sending the tingling message of a warm togetherness that wasn't true. Cole was her boss. He would do her the courtesy of accompanying her to her door and then he would leave her. Back to business on Monday.

She put her head down and walked, acutely conscious of the sound of their footsteps—the quick clacking of her heels, the slower thump of his. They seemed to echo through the emptiness of her personal life, mocking dreams that had never been fulfilled, recalling her mother's words—*The kind of man you want, Liz, is the marrying kind.*

Why couldn't she meet someone who was?

Want someone who was.

Someone who was at least…reachable!

Tears blurred her eyes as they started up the stairs to her apartment. She shouldn't have drunk those glasses of champagne, giving her a false high, making the down worse. It was paramount now that she pull herself together, get out her door key, formulate a polite goodbye to her boss who had done her many kindnesses today. Kind…generous…making her feel special…

A huge lump rose in her throat. She blinked, swallowed, blinked, swallowed, managed somehow to get the key in the lock, turned it, pushed the door open enough for a fast getaway, retrieved the key, dropped it in her bag, dragged a deep breath into her aching chest, and turned to the man beside her.

'Thank you for everything, Cole,' she recited stiltedly and tried to arrange her mouth into a smile as she lifted her gaze, knowing she had to briefly meet his eyes and desperately hoping no evidence of any excess moisture was left for him to see. 'Goodnight,' she added as brightly as she could. 'It was fun.'

Cole's whole body clenched, resisting the dismissal. He stared at her shiny eyes. Wet eyes. Green pools, reflecting deep misery. The smile she'd forced was quivering, falling apart, no fun left to keep it in a natural curve.

He should let her go.

They were on very private ground now.

If he crossed it, there'd be no going back.

She was his employee…

Yet he stepped forward, his body responding to a primal tug that flouted the reasonable workings of his mind. Raising a hand, he gently stroked the tremulous corner of her mouth, wanting to soothe, to comfort, to make her feel safe with him. A slight gasp whispered from her lips. Her eyes swam with a terrible vulnerability, fearful questions begging to be answered.

It laid a responsibility on him, instantly striking a host of male instincts that rose in a strangely exultant wave, urging him to fight, to hold, to take, to protect—the age-old role of man before current day society had watered it down into something much less.

A sense of dominant power surged through his veins. She would submit to it. He would draw a positive response from her. He sensed it waiting behind the fear and confusion, waiting to be ignited, to flare into hot fusion with the desire pounding through him.

He slid his hand over her cheek, felt the leap of warmth under her skin, the firm yet fragile line of her jaw, the delicate curl of her small ear. Even as his thumb tilted her chin, his fingers were reaching to the nape of her neck, ready to caress, to persuade, to possess.

He lowered his head...slowly, savouring the moment of impact before it came. She had time to break away. His hold on her was light. She stood still, as though her entire being was poised for this first intimate contact with him, caught up in a breathless anticipation that couldn't be turned aside.

His lips touched hers, settling over their softness, drawing on them with light sips, feeling their hesitant response, teasing them into a more open kiss, wanting an exchange of sensation, reining in the urge to plunder and devour. She was willing to experiment, her tongue tentatively touching his as though she wasn't sure this was right. It fired a fierce desire in Cole to convince her it was. He turned the kiss into a slow, sensual dance, intent on melting every inhibition. She followed his lead, seduced into playing his game, savouring it herself, beginning to like it, want it, initiating as well as responding.

Excitement kicked through Cole. This was so different to Tara's all-too-knowing sexual aggression. He had to win this woman, drive the memory of her lost partner out of her mind and supplant it with what *he* could make her feel. The challenge spurred him into sweeping her into his embrace.

Her spine stiffened, whether in shock or resistance he didn't know. Shock was probably good. Resistance was bad. Before he could blast it with a passionate onslaught of kisses, her palms pressed hard against his chest and her head pulled back from his—a warning against force that he struggled to check, sensing her need for choice here, even while gathering himself to sway it his way.

He felt the agitated heave of her breasts as she sucked in a quick breath. Her lids fluttered, lashes half veiling the eloquent confusion in her eyes. Satisfaction welled in him, despite the frustration of being halted. It wasn't rejection on her mind. She didn't understand what was going on in his.

'Why are you doing this?' The words spilled out, anxious, frightened of consequences that he should know as well as she.

The lack of any calculation in her question, the sheer exquisite innocence of it evoked a streak of tenderness that Cole would have sworn had died with his son. His own chest heaved with the sudden surge of emotion. He dropped a soft kiss on her forehead.

'Because it feels right,' he murmured, feeling the sense of a new beginning so strongly, his heart started racing at the possibility it was really true. He could move past Tara. Even past David. Perhaps it was only hope but he wasn't about to step away from this opportunity of taking a future track which might bring him all he'd craved in his darkest nights.

'But I'm not really a…a date, am I?' she argued, trying to get a handle on what he meant by kissing her.

'No. You're much more.'

She shook her head, not comprehending. 'Cole, please…' Anguished uncertainty in her eyes. '…we have to work together.'

'We do work together. That's precisely the point. We work very well together.' He stroked the worry line between her brows. 'I'm just taking it to another level.'

'Another level?' she repeated dazedly.

He smiled into her eyes, wanting to dispel the cloudiness, to make her see what he saw. 'This feels right to me, Liz. Don't let it feel wrong to you because it's not,' he insisted, recklessly intent on carrying her with him. On a wild burst of adrenalin he added, 'I'm damned sure I can give you more than Brendan ever could or would.'

'Bren…dan.'

The name seemed to confuse her further. Cole silently cursed himself for bringing it up. He didn't want to compete. He wanted to conquer—wipe the guy out, take the woman, make her his. He didn't care how primitive that course was. It burned in his gut and he acted on it, sweeping Liz with him into her apartment, closing the door, staking his claim on her territory.

Before she could even think of protesting, he threw off his leather jacket, needing no armour against the cold in here, nor any barrier to the enticing heat of her body, and he captured her within the lock of his arms, intent on her surrender to his will. She felt small against him, and all the more intensely feminine because of it, but he knew she had a backbone of steel that could defy the might of his physique. Triumph zinged through his brain as her spine softened, arched into him, and her hands slid up over his shoulders, around his neck, and she lifted herself on tiptoe, face tilted to his, ready to be kissed again.

The darkness of the room seemed to sharpen his

senses. He could smell her perfume, enticingly erotic. His fingers wove through the silky curls of her hair, revelling in the tactile pleasure of it. His body hardened to the yielding softness of hers. He was conscious of their breaths mingling as his mouth touched hers, touched and clung with a voracious need that demanded her compliance.

She kissed him back with a passionate defiance that challenged any sense of dominance over her. No submission. It was as though a fire had erupted in her and Cole caught the flame. It flared through him, firing his desire for her to furnace heat. The power of it raced out of control, taking them both, drawing them in, sucking them towards the intense thrill of merging so completely there could be no turning back.

He removed her jacket.

She lifted his sweater, fearless now in matching him step for step.

Discarding clothes…like walls coming down, crashing to the floor, opening up the way…the ravenous excitement of flesh meeting flesh, sliding, caressing, hot and hungry for more and more intimacy.

Kissing…like nothing he knew, sliding deep, a sensual mating of tongues, a fierce response generated in every cell of his body, the sense of immense strength, power humming.

He scooped her off her feet, cradled her against his chest, carried her, intuitively picking the route to the room where she had gone to get her scarf this morning. Her head rested on his shoulder, her face pressed to his neck, the whole feel of her soft and warm and womanly, giving, wanting what he wanted.

She made him feel as a man should feel.

Essentially male.

And all that entailed.

CHAPTER ELEVEN

LIZ was glad of the darkness. It wasn't oppressive now. It was her friend and ally, heightening the vibrant reality of Cole making love to her while it hid the same reality in comforting shadows. It allowed her to stifle the fear of facing the sheer nakedness of what they were doing and revel in the incredible pleasure of it. She could even believe she was as desirable as Cole made her feel. In the darkness.

He laid her on the bed—a bed she had shared only with Brendan—and she felt a sharp inner recoil at the memory, not wanting it. Why had Cole referred to him? Brendan was gone. Long gone from her bed. And he'd made mincemeat of her heart—the heart that was now pounding with wild excitement as Cole loomed over her, so big and strong and dynamically male, as different as any man could be to Brendan.

Purpose…action…energy focused on carrying through decisions…and unbelievably that focus was now on her…a totally irresistible force that kept swamping the reservations that should be in her brain, but he'd blown them away as though they didn't count. And maybe they didn't at this level, wherever this level was taking them.

She could barely think. Couldn't reason anymore. His arms slid out from under her and the solid mass of him straightened up, substance not fantasy, Cole

123

taking charge, wanting her with him like this. She saw his arm reach for the bedside lamp and reacted with violent rejection of the action he had in mind.

'No!'

The arm was momentarily checked. 'No what?' he demanded.

'No light. I don't want light.'

'Why not?'

'You'll see…'

'I want to see you.'

'It won't be right,' she argued desperately. Her mind was screaming, *I'm not built like Tara. My breasts are small. My legs aren't long. I don't have voluptuous curves.*

'I promise you it will be,' he said, his voice furred with a deep sensuality that did promise, yet she couldn't believe he wouldn't compare her body to that of the woman he'd married and find her wanting.

'I don't have red hair down there,' she cried frantically, clutching at anything to stop him from turning on the light. 'You'll see it and think of me as a little brown mouse again.'

'I never thought of you like that,' he growled. 'Never!'

It got him onto the bed, lying beside her, the lamp forgotten, his hand sliding down over her stomach, fingers thrusting into the tight curls below it. 'I always saw you as bright, Liz Hart. Bright eyes. Bright intelligence. And behind it a fire which occasionally leapt out at me. There's not an ounce of mouse in you.'

This emphatic string of statements was very reassuring as to her status in his eyes, but Liz was highly distracted from it by the further glide of his fingers, delving lower, probing soft sensitive folds, exciting nerve ends that melted into slick heat.

'I thought this past week...she's showing her true colours. Reflecting the real Liz instead of covering her up,' he went on, still wreaking exquisite havoc with his hand, caressing, tracing, teasing. 'You don't need a cloak of darkness. You can't hide from me anymore. I know the fire inside you. I can feel it...'

A finger slid inside the entrance to her body and tantalisingly circled the sensitive inner wall, raising convulsive quivers of anticipation for the ultimate act of intimacy. He leaned over, his face hovering above hers. She saw the flash of a smile.

'...and taste it.'

He kissed her, long and deeply, and the tantalising fingertip plunged inward, stroking in the same rhythmic action as his tongue, a dual invasion that drove her wild with passionate need, a need that swelled inside her, arching her body in an instinctive lift towards his, wanting, yearning. He didn't instantly respond so she reached for him with her hands, turned towards him, threw a leg over his, and her heart leapt at the hard muscular strength it met. Huge thighs. She'd forgotten how big he was, had a moment's trepidation...how would it be when he took her?

I promise you it will be right...

It had to be.

She didn't want to stop.

Not now.

Not when she was awash with a tumultuous

need to have him…if only this once. It was madness…dangerous madness…risking what should have been kept safe. But it was his choice. *She* was his choice. And feeling him wanting her—Cole Pierson wanting her—it was like being elevated above any other woman he could have had, above Tara, making her feel…marvellous!

He broke the kiss and moved, but not as she expected, craved. His mouth fastened over the pulse at the base of her throat, radiating a heat that suffused her entire skin. She heard herself panting, barely able to breathe. Her arms had locked around his neck, but his head slipped below their circle, his lips tracing the upper swell of one breast, shifting to its tip…

Her stomach contracted as the feeling of inadequacy attacked her again. Her breasts weren't lush. He'd be disappointed in them. Oh, why, why couldn't he just…

Sensation exploded through her as he drew the tense peak into the hot wetness of his mouth and sucked on it. Swept it with his tongue. Another rhythmic assault that moved in tandem with the caressing hand between her thighs, driving her to the edge of shattering. Her fingers scrabbled blindly in his hair, pressing, tugging, protesting, inciting.

He moved to her other breast, increasing her ache for him, and her flesh seemed to swell around his mouth, throbbing with a tight fullness that totally erased any concern about levels of femininity. He made her feel she was all the woman he wanted and he wouldn't be denied any part of her.

Again he shifted and her body jerked as his tongue

swirled around her navel, a hot sweep of kisses trailing lower, lower. Her hands grabbed ineffectually at the bunched muscles of his shoulders as fear and desire warred through her mind.

No hesitation in his. Ruthless purpose. Lips pressed to her curls, fingers parting the way, his tongue touching, licking. The intensity of feeling rocked her, drenched her with desire, rendered her utterly helpless to stop anything even if she'd wanted to. And she didn't. She was on fire and he was tasting her because he wanted to.

He wedged his shoulders between her thighs, lifted her legs, clamped his hands on her hips and held her fast as he replaced the caress of his hand with the incredibly intimate caress of his mouth, his lips encircling her, his tongue probing with such artful sensual skill, she couldn't breathe at all as the intensity of feeling grew, ripping through her. She tried to ride the tide of it, her hands gripping the bedcover, holding on, holding on, but a rush of heat broke through her inner walls, overwhelming her with a wave of excruciating delight. A cry broke from her throat as she lost all sense of self, falling into a deep well of pleasure that engulfed her in sweet, molten heat.

Then Cole was surging over her. She could see him, feel him, but her muscles were so limp, she was unable to react. Her mind was filled with awe that he had taken her this far before satisfying himself. Yet she sensed he was not unsatisfied with what he had done, but pleased, even triumphant, as though he'd found his feasting very much to his liking.

I promise you it will be right...

Impossible to deny it, feeling as she did.

Having set himself to enter her, he pressed forward, pushing into her slowly, letting her adjust to the thick fullness of him, a completely different sensation and one that re-electrified all her senses. He eased back, lifting her hips, stuffing a pillow under her.

'Put your legs around me,' he murmured.

Somehow she managed to do it, locking her ankles so that they wouldn't slip apart. This time his thrust was firm, pushing deep, deeper, filling her to a breathtaking depth, then bracing himself on his arms as he bent his head to join his mouth to hers, and the kiss was different, too, like an absolute affirmation of him being inside her, having him there, an intensely felt sensation of possessing and being possessed, exulting in it, absorbed by it.

'Now rock with me,' he instructed, flashing a smile as he lifted his head.

Joy rippled through her. He was happy with where they were. She was, too. It re-energised her body, making it easy now to move as he did, matching the repetitive undulation, even touching him, stroking him, encouraging him, running her hands over the warm skin of his back, inciting the rise of heat with each delicious rhythmic plunge.

It was a wild, primitive dance that she gloried in, flesh sliding against—into—flesh, fusing, yet still gliding with a strong, relentless purpose, friction building to ecstatic peaks, wave after wave of intense sensation rolling through her…so much to feel…flaring, swirling, pooling deep inside her, touching her heart, stirring indefinable emotions…too much to pin down…far beyond all her previous experience.

Rapture as he groaned and spilled himself inside her. She sighed his name as his hard body collapsed on her, spent, and she wrapped her arms around him, holding him close, loving him, owning him if only for these few precious moments in time. He'd given himself to her, all that he was, and she silently revelled in the gift, unable to see ahead to what came next, not caring, listening to his heart thundering, elated that he had reached a pinnacle of pleasure with her.

He raised himself to kiss her again, her name whispering from his lips as they covered hers, soft, lingering sips that demanded nothing, merely sealing a tender togetherness that tasted of true and total contentment. Then his arms burrowed under her and he rolled onto his back, carrying her with him so that she lay with her head under his chin, her body sprawled over his.

Done, she thought, and wondered where it would lead. But with no sense of anxiety. She felt too amazingly replete to worry about tomorrow. Only luxuriating in this blissful sense of peace mattered. As long as it lasted. It awed her that she had lived so many years without realising how fantastic intimacy could be with a man. With the right man. Cole…Cole Pierson. Was it asking too much to want him thinking the same about her?

Probably it was.

This could be just a timing thing with him—a backlash against Tara's assumption that she could rope him in again, making the alleged intimacy between him and his personal assistant real because it had been planted in his mind, and it was an act of defiance against any desire he might have left for his almost ex-wife.

People did do reckless things on the rebound.

Was he thinking of Tara now…mentally thumbing his nose at her?

Liz felt herself growing cold at these thoughts and fiercely set them aside. Cole was with her. He'd chosen her. She moved her hand, suddenly wanting to stoke his desire again, feel it burning through her, obliterating everything else with the intense sense of possession.

A long sensual caress from his armpit, down his rib-cage, over the hollows underneath his hipbones, his firm flesh quivering to her touch, pleasured by it. She levered herself to a lower position so she could close her mouth over his nipple, kissing it, lashing it with her tongue. His chest heaved, dragging in a sharp breath, reacting swiftly to the sexual energy that had roared around them and was sparking again, gathering momentum.

She reached further, her hand closing around him, fondling, stroking. He groaned, his whole body tensing as her thumb brushed delicately over the sensitive head of his shaft. Elated at his response, she seized him more firmly, felt the surge of rampant strength grow hard, harder…

Hands gripped her waist, lifting her. 'Straddle me,' came the gravelled command. 'Put me inside you.'

It was an even more incredible sensation, lowering

herself onto him, engineering the penetration herself, feeling her inner muscles convulse and adjust to the pressing fullness of him, loving the sense of taking him, owning him. His hands moved to her hips, helping her sink further as he raised his thighs behind her, forming a cradle for her bottom, a cradle he rocked to breathtaking effect.

'Lean forward.'

She wanted to anyway, wanted to kiss him as he'd kissed her when he was deep inside her. She placed her hands on his shoulders and merged her mouth with his, plunging into a cavern of wild passion, drawn into a whirlpool of need that he answered with ravishing speed, his hands on her everywhere, stroking, shaping, kneading, strong fingers clutching, gentle fingers loving, sensitising every inch of her flesh to his touch.

She lifted herself back and he rubbed his palms over her nipples, rotating the hardened buds, exciting them almost beyond bearing, then latching onto them one by one with his mouth, his hands back on her hips, moving her from side to side, up and down, stirring a frenzy of sensation that rocketed through her, shattering every last vestige of control.

Even as she started to collapse on him he caught her face, drew it down to his, and devoured her mouth again, a sweet devastating plunder that she could only surrender to, helplessly yet willingly because the intoxication of his desire for more and more of her was too strong an exhilaration to deny.

Then amazingly, he was surging upright, swinging his legs off the bed, holding her pinned to him across his lap, hugging her tightly, her breasts crushed so intimately against his chest, the beat of his heart seemed to pound through them, echoing the throb of her own. And he remained inside her, a glorious sensual fullness, as his fingers wound through her hair and his lips grazed over her ear.

'I have never felt anything as good as this,' he murmured, his voice furred with a wonderment that squeezed her heart and sent elation soaring through her bloodstream. He tilted her head back, rained kisses over her face, her forehead, her eyelids, her cheeks, his lips hovering over hers as he added with compelling urgency, 'Tell me it's so for you. Tell me.'

'Yes.' The word spilled out automatically, impossible not to concede the truth, and he captured it in his mouth and carried it into hers, exploding the force of it with a fierce enthralling passion, holding her caged in his arms, swaying to reinforce the sense of his other insertion, pressing the heated walls of the passage he filled, making her feel him with commanding intensity.

'So, good, it has to be right,' he said rawly as he broke the kiss and cupped her chin, his eyes burning into hers. 'So don't you doubt it tomorrow. Or on Monday. Or anytime in the future.'

Emphatic words, punching into her dazed mind. She wasn't sure what he was saying. Her brain formed its own message. 'Right…for one night,' she sighed, knowing she would never forget the feelings he'd aroused in her, was still arousing. She didn't care if it was only one experience. It was the experience of a lifetime.

'No.' His hands raked through her hair, pressing for concentration. 'This isn't an end. It's a beginning. You and me, Liz. Moving forward, moving together. Feel it. Know it. Come with me.'

He moved his thighs, driving an acute awareness of their sexual connection. He was still strongly erect, probing her inmost self, demanding she yield to him, and what else could she do? She wanted this deeper bonding, wanted it to last far beyond now.

'Liz...' An urgent demand poured through her name.

She lifted her limp, heavy arms and locked them around his neck...for better or worse, she thought, her mind aswim, drowning in the need for Cole to keep wanting her, making her feel loved as a woman.

'Yes.' It was the only word humming through her mind. Yes to anything, everything with him.

'Yes-s-s...' he echoed, but with a ring of triumphant satisfaction, powerfully realised.

One hand skated down the curve of her spine, curled under the soft globes of her bottom, clasping her to him as he rose to his feet and turned to lower her onto the bed again, her head and shoulders resting on the coverlet as he dragged pillows under her hips, then knelt between the spread of her legs, leaning over her, hands intertwining with hers, a wild grin of joy on his face.

'We'll both come,' he promised wickedly, then began to thrust in a fast driving beat, rocking deeply into her, and she felt her body receive him with an exultant welcome, opening to him over and over again. And he claimed all she gave, imprinting himself so completely on her consciousness, her entire body was focused on the erotic friction he built and built…only pausing, becoming still when he felt the powerful ripples of her release, savouring them before he picked up the rhythm again, all restraint whipping away as he pursued his own climax, broken breaths, moans of mounting tension, climbing, climbing, bursting into a long, intense rapture, waves of heat spilling, swirling, fusing them, lifting them into a space where they floated together in ecstatic harmony.

And Liz no longer questioned anything.

A sense of perfect contentment reigned.

Sliding slowly and languorously into a feast of sensuality that lasted long into the night…the night that he said was a beginning, not an end.

CHAPTER TWELVE

COLE was gone when Liz awoke. She vaguely remembered him kissing her, murmuring he had to keep an appointment. He'd been fully clothed, ready to leave. She was almost sure she'd mumbled, 'Okay,' before dropping back into a heavy sleep.

It came as a shock that her bedside radio now showed 11:47, almost midday. There was only one afternoon of the weekend left and she had washing to do, food shopping. She bolted out of bed and headed straight into the bathroom, cold wintry air hitting her nakedness, making her shiver.

A hot shower dispelled the chill and soaping her body brought back all the memories of last night's intimacies with Cole…delicious, indelible memories. If she wasn't in love with the man, she was certainly in lust with him. He was an incredible lover. And he'd made her feel sexier than she'd ever felt in her life. Sexy, beautiful, special…

Her mind flitted to how it had been with Brendan. Why had she accepted *so little* from him? Compared to Cole…but she hadn't known any better at the time. In fact, Brendan had been mean about a lot of things—a taker, not a giver. Whereas Cole…the beautiful clothes yesterday, the sumptuous dinner last night, the loving…she felt wonderfully spoilt, as though all her Christmases had come at once.

She desperately hoped it *was* right to have plunged into this intimate relationship with him. Her job was very definitely at risk if it turned wrong. Oddly enough, work security didn't weigh so heavily on her mind now. Losing him would be far more devastating. Which was the problem with being raised to giddy heights. The fall…

But she wasn't going to think about that.

Nor was she going to worry about Cole being her boss. As Diana had predicted, *he* had done the running, and Liz was now determined on *going with the flow,* wherever it took her. There really was no other choice, except dropping entirely out of his life. And why would she do that when he made her feel…so good?

The somewhat sobering recollection slid into her mind—he was in no hurry to marry again.

So what? she quickly argued. Did she have any prospects leaping out at her? Not a one. Besides, there was no guarantee of permanence with any relationship. It went that way or it didn't. Though everything within her craved for this new relationship with Cole to last, to become truly solid, to have it fulfil…all her impossible dreams.

As she stepped out of the shower, dried herself and dressed, a wry little smile lingered on her lips. Perhaps hope *was* eternal. In any event, it was a happy boost to her spirits. So was emptying yesterday's shopping bags, remembering the zing of parading the clothes in front of Cole as she hung them up in her wardrobe, knowing now that he did see her as a desirable woman—a woman he wanted.

She rushed through the afternoon, doing all the necessary chores, planning what she'd pack for the trip with Cole's mother, making sure everything was clean, ready to wear. She wondered what Nancy would think of her son becoming attached to his personal assistant. Better me than Tara, Liz cheerfully decided. Nancy hadn't liked Tara at all.

She was still riding a high when her telephone rang just past seven o'clock. She hesitated over answering it, thinking it might be Diana with another stream of advice. She didn't want to share what had happened with Cole. Not yet. It suddenly felt too precious, too fragile. And she didn't know how it might be tomorrow.

On the other hand, it might be her mother who wasn't pushing anything, only for her daughter to be happy about herself, and Liz was happy about herself right now, so she snatched up the receiver and spoke with a smile. 'Hi! Liz here.'

'Cole here,' came the lilted reply, warm pleasure threading his voice.

'Oh!' A dumb response but he'd taken her by surprise.

'Oh good, I trust?'

The light teasing note brought the smile back. 'Yes. Definitely good.'

He laughed. 'I've been thinking of you all day. Highly distracting.'

'Should I say I'm sorry?' It was fun to flirt with him, though it amazed her that she could.

'No. The distraction was very pleasurable.' He drawled the last words, sending pinpricks of excitement all over her skin. 'I'm currently having to restrain myself from dashing to your door, telling myself I do need some sleep in order to function well tomorrow.'

'You have a string of meetings in the morning,' she said primly, playing the perfect P.A. while inwardly delighted that his restraint was being tested. It spoke volumes about the strength of attraction he felt. Towards *her*.

'Mmmh…I was wondering how to alleviate the problem of people getting in the way of us.'

Us…such an exhilarating word. 'We do have work to get through, Cole,' she reminded him, though if he didn't care, she wasn't about to care, either.

'True. But you could wear that bronze dress with the buttons down the front. Very provocative those buttons. One could say…promising.'

Liz felt her thighs pressing together, recapturing the sensations of last night when he'd…

'And wear stockings,' he continued. 'Not those coverall pantihose. Stockings that end mid-thigh, under the skirt with the buttons. And no one will know but you and me, Liz. I like that idea. I like it very much.'

His voice had dropped to a seductive purr, and her entire body was reacting to it, an exquisite squirming that actually curled her toes.

'If you'll do that I think I'm sure to perform at a high peak tomorrow,' he went on, conjuring up breathtaking images that dizzied her brain. 'Won't feel deprived at all during those meetings. There's nothing quite like waiting on a promise.'

A shiver ran down her spine. Did he mean...after the meetings...at the office? He wanted sex with her there?

'Liz?'

'Yes?' It was like punching air out her lungs.

'Have I shocked you?'

'Yes...no,' she gabbled. 'I mean...I wasn't sure what you'd want of me tomorrow.'

'You. I want you. In every way there is,' he answered with a strength of purpose that thudded straight into Liz's heart, making her feeling intensely vulnerable about how he would deal with her in the end if she trod this path with him. Was it only sex on his mind? How much did she count as a person?

She couldn't find anything to say, her mind riddled by doubts and fears, yet physically, sexually, she was aware of an overwhelming yearning to follow his lead, to be the woman he wanted in every way.

'Remember how right it felt?' he dropped into her silence.

'Yes,' she answered huskily, her voice barely rising over a huge emotional lump in her throat.

'It will be tomorrow, too. That's my promise, Liz.' Warm reassurance.

'I'll come as you say,' she decided recklessly.

'Good! I'll sleep on that. Sweet dreams.'

The connection clicked off.

Goal achieved, she thought, then shook her head dazedly over the power Cole Pierson could and did exert. Being the focus of it was like nothing she had ever known before. In the past, she had always done the running, not very effectually where men were concerned. No truly satisfying success at all. In actual fact, a string of failures, probably because she'd tried to manage things to turn out right instead of them just being right.

She had no control with Cole.

He'd seized it.

Was still wielding it.

And maybe that was how it should be.

So let it be.

Cole sat at his desk in his office, his computer switched on, the screen flashing figures he should be checking, but he was too much on tenterhooks, waiting for Liz to arrive. He couldn't remember ever being this tense about seeing a woman again. Would he win or lose on last night's gamble?

He wasn't sure of her.

The sex on Saturday night had been fantastic. No doubting her response to everything they'd done together—a more than willing partner in pleasure, once he'd moved her past the initial inhibitions—storming barriers before she could raise them. Barriers that had undoubtedly been built during the Brendan era—damage done by a selfish lover who didn't have the sense to appreciate the woman he had.

Cole knew he could definitely reach her on the sexual level. It was what he was counting on to bind her to him. He'd moved too fast to take a slower route now, and be damned if he was going to let her slip away from him. He'd sensed her second thoughts during the telephone call. Perhaps the better move would have been to stay with her all yesterday. But her apartment was her ground and she would have had the right to ask him to go.

Best to keep the initiative.

She'd come to work this morning—his ground. And after their conversation over the phone, she would have gone to bed last night thinking of him, tempted by the promise of more pleasure, remembering what they'd already shared, wanting more...

Cole dragged in a deep breath, trying to dampen the wild surge of desire rising at the thought of what she would wear today. Compliance or defiance? At least the signal would be clear, the moment she walked into his office. Yes...no. He fiercely willed it to be yes. And why not? She had the fire in her to pursue pleasure. He'd lit the flame. She wouldn't let it go out...would she?

A knock on his door.

'Come in!' he called, his voice too terse, on edge.

She stepped into his office, wearing the bronze dress with the buttons down the front.

His heart thundered as a lightning burst of triumph flashed through his mind.

'Good morning,' she said brightly.

He saw courage in the red flags on her cheeks, in the high tilt of her head, the squared shoulders, the smile that wavered slightly at its corners. Courage defying fear and uncertainty. It touched him to a surprising depth.

'I think it's a great morning,' he rolled out, his smile ablaze with admiration and approval.

She visibly relaxed, walking forward, holding out

a Manila folder. 'I brought in the file for your first meeting.'

Straight into business.

Not quite yet, Cole thought. 'I seem to remember that the last time I saw you in that dress, there were several buttons towards the hem undone.'

It was a challenging reminder and she halted, looking down at her skirt in hot confusion.

'Three,' he said. 'I recall counting three undone.'

Her gaze lifted, eyes astonished. 'You counted them?'

He grinned. 'I'm good at counting.'

A little laugh gurgled from her throat. 'So you are.'

'And here you are all buttoned up today, which doesn't look right at all. I much preferred it the other way. I think you should oblige me and undo at least one button before we get down to serious business.'

'One button,' she repeated, her eyes sparkling at the mischievous nonsense.

Fun was the key here. There was never enough fun in anyone's life. She'd had fun trying clothes on during the buying spree on Saturday. What could be more relaxing and seductive than having fun with some knowingly provocative undressing?

'Okay. One button for now,' he agreed. 'Though I think it would relieve the pressure of these meetings if an extra button got undone after each session.'

'That makes four buttons.'

'I knew you were good at counting, too.'

She gave him an arch look, joining in the game he was playing. 'You might find that distracting.'

'No. I'll think of it as my reward for outstanding concentration.'

She placed the folder on the desk. Then with an air of whimsical indulgence, she flicked open the bottom button, straightened up, took a deep breath and boldly asked, 'Happy now?'

'We progress. Let's say I'm…briefly…satisfied.' He ran his gaze up the row of buttons from hem to neckline, then smiled, meeting her eyes with deliberately wicked intent.

She flushed, realising he had no intention of stopping anywhere. *And may she burn with anticipation all morning,* Cole thought as he drew the folder over to his side of the desk and opened it, ostensibly ready to familiarise himself with the financial details of the client who would soon be arriving.

He'd thrown his net, caught Liz with it, and he'd draw her closer and closer to him as the morning wore on. The whole encounter had sharpened his mind brilliantly. He felt right on top of the game.

An hour later, the first client had been dealt with. Without saying a word, Cole stared at Liz's skirt. Without a word from her, she undid a button, then handed him the next file.

Exhilarated by the silent complicity, Cole ploughed through the next meeting, sparking on all cylinders.

Another button hit the dust.

He could see above her knee now when she walked, the skirt peeping open far enough to tease him with flashes of leg. Was she wearing stockings as he'd requested?

Excitement buzzed through his brain. Restraint was

like a refined torture. He forced it over the desire simmering through him and satisfied the third client with a fast and comprehensive exposition on the state of the money markets. Even as he ushered the man out of his office, his gaze targeted the next button, wanting it opened, commanding it done...now...this instant.

He saw her hands move to do it as he walked his client through Liz's office. Anticipation roared through him. It was an act of will to keep accompanying the man to the elevator, farewelling him into the compartment before turning back to the woman who had to be wanting an acceleration of action as much as he did.

He'd planned the sexual tease. He'd meant it to go on all day, but here he was, too caught up with the need it had evoked in him to wait for tonight. To hell with work. It was lunch time anyway. Though his appetite for Liz Hart wiped out any thought of food. The energy driving him now did not require more fuel.

He strode into her office, locked the door against any possible interruption. She stood at one of the filing cabinets, putting the last folder away. The click of the lock caused her to throw a startled glance over her shoulder. Their eyes met, the sizzling intent in his causing hers to widen.

'It's all right,' he said, soothing any shock. 'We're alone. Private. And I want you very urgently, Liz Hart.'

She didn't move, seemingly entranced by the force of need emanating from him. Then he was behind her, his arms caging her, pulling her back against him, finding some solace for his fierce erection in pressing it against the soft cleft of her sexy bottom.

He heard, felt her gasp, kissed the delicate nape of her neck, needing to give vent to the storm of desire engulfing him. He was so hungry for her. His hands covered her stomach, pushing in, making her feel how much he wanted her. Then he remembered the buttons, stockings, bare thighs, and his desire for her took another turn. He dropped his hands, fingers moving swiftly, opening the skirt.

And yes, yes...it was how he'd envisaged, stockings ending, naked flesh above them, quivering to his touch, the crotch of her panties hot, moist, telling evidence of her excitement, boosting his.

He whirled her over to her desk, sat her on it, took her chair, spread her legs, lifting them over his shoulders as he bent to taste the soft, bare, tremulous inner walls of her thighs, kissing, licking, smelling her need for him, exulting in it, knowing she was his to take as he wanted.

Liz could hardly believe what was happening. He was spreading the silk of her panties tight, kissing her through the thin screen, finding the throbbing centre between her folds, sucking on it. Pleasure rushed from the heat of his mouth, sweeping through her like a tidal wave. She had to lie back on the desk to cope with it, though there was no coping, more a melting surrender to the flow of sensation.

And she had once thought him an ice man!

He let her legs slide from his shoulders as he rose,

seemingly intent on following her, bending over her, his eyes dark, ringed with burning blue—no ice!— and she felt the silk being drawn aside as the hot hard length of him pushed to possess the space waiting for him, aching for him.

The intense focus of his eyes captured hers, held it as he drove the penetration home. 'This is how it is…in the light,' he said raggedly. 'You don't need the dark, Liz. It's better this way, seeing, knowing…'

He withdrew enough to plunge again, and it *was* thrilling to see the tension on his face, the concentrated flare of desire in his eyes, to watch him moving in the driving rhythm that pleasured them both in ever increasing pulse beats of intense excitement. The final release was incredibly mutual, and instinctively she wrapped her arms around his head and drew his mouth to hers, kissing him with the sweet knowledge that his desire for her was very real, not some accident of fate because she was simply on hand at a time of need.

This was proven to her over and over again as the days—and nights—rolled on towards the date of departure for the trip to South-East Asia. For the most part, restraint ruled in the office, but then they would go to her apartment, his apartment, make wild needy love, proceed to a nearby restaurant for dinner, enjoy fine food and wine while they whetted their appetite for more lovemaking.

It was exhilarating, addictive, a whirlwind of un-inhibited passion, and Liz was so completely caught up in it, she heartily wished she wasn't going off travelling with his mother…until Cole made an announcement over dinner on Thursday night that gave her pause for thought.

'My divorce was settled this afternoon. I'm finally a free man again.'

It was the relief in his voice that unsettled her, as though his freedom had remained threatened until the law had brought his marriage to Tara Summerville to an end. It instantly brought to mind the confrontation between them last Saturday, with Tara firing all her guns to win a reconciliation, and Cole savagely denying her any chance of it.

Since then—apart from Sunday when he had been occupied elsewhere—he had virtually immersed himself in a white-hot affair with the very woman Tara had accused of a sexual connection to Cole. Had it become so concentrated in order to keep Tara completely shut out? No space for her, not in his mind, not in his life, ensuring the final line was drawn on a marriage he'd written off as a case of bad judgment.

One could settle things in one's head that didn't necessarily get translated into physical and emotional responses. In a kind of reverse situation, Liz knew she'd reasoned out a million things about Brendan, trying to keep positive about their relationship, even when her body and heart were reacting negatively. The old saying, mind over matter, didn't really work. It only covered over stuff that kept bubbling underneath.

Liz couldn't help wondering if Cole had chosen her as the best possible distraction to take him through to the finishing line with Tara. Yet the sexual chemistry they shared had to be real. He couldn't perform as he did unless he felt it. And he'd noticed how many buttons had been undone on the bronze dress last week, before that meeting with Tara. Which surely meant Liz could trust the attraction between them.

It was just that Cole had such a formidable mind. Once he decided something, he went at it full bore until the goal was achieved. And Liz didn't know what his goal was with her, except to satisfy a very strong sexual urge—made right because she wanted the same satisfaction. Although secretly she wanted more from him. Much more.

But nothing was said about any future with.her. Too soon, Liz told herself. After dinner, Cole drove her home. This was their last night together for more than two weeks while she toured through South-East Asia with his mother. She had Friday off to pack and generally get ready for the trip so she wouldn't be seeing him at work tomorrow. It had been arranged for her to meet Nancy Pierson at the airport Holiday Inn at six o'clock for a tour group dinner and they would fly off early Saturday morning.

Cole stayed late, seemingly reluctant to part from her even when he finally chose to leave. 'I wish you weren't going on this trip,' he said with a rueful smile, then kissed her long and hard, passionately reminding her of all the intimacy they'd shared. 'I'll miss you,' he murmured against her lips.

In every sense, Liz hoped, silently deciding the trip was a timely break, giving them both the distance to reflect on what they'd done, where they were going with it and why.

She felt she'd been caught up in a fever-pitch compulsion that completely blotted out everything else beyond Cole Pierson. Distance might give her enough perspective to see if it truly was good...or the result of influences that had pulled them somewhere they shouldn't be.

Which wouldn't be good at all.

CHAPTER THIRTEEN

BY MIDAFTERNOON Friday, Cole found himself totally irritated by the temporary assistant taking Liz's place. He wasn't asking much of her. Why did she have to look so damned intimidated all the time? He hoped his mother appreciated the sacrifice he was making, giving her Liz as a companion for this trip.

Which reminded him to call his mother before the limousine arrived to transport her to the airport Holiday Inn, make sure she wasn't in a tizz about having everything ready to go. He picked up the telephone and dialled the number for the Palm Beach house.

'Yes?' his mother answered breathlessly.

'Just calm down, Mum. The limousine can wait until you're sure you haven't left anything behind.'

'Oh, Cole! I was just going around the house to check everything was locked.'

'I'll drive out tomorrow and double-check the security alarm so don't worry about it. Okay?'

A big sigh. 'Thank you, dear. There's always so much to think about before I leave. I did call your Liz and she assured me she's all organised.'

His Liz. A pity she wasn't his right now. In more ways than one. 'She would be,' he said dryly.

'Such a nice girl!' came the voice of warm approval. 'I rather hope we do run into her boyfriend at

Kathmandu. I can't imagine he's not having second thoughts about leaving her.'

'What?' The word squawked out of the shock that momentarily paralysed Cole's brain.

'You must know about him,' his mother said reasonably. 'Brendan Wheeler. He and Liz have been together for the past three years.'

'Yes, I know about him,' Cole snapped. 'But not that he was in Kathmandu. When did Liz tell you this?'

'Last Saturday when we were working out what clothes to take. It seemed wrong that she didn't have a boyfriend, so I asked her...'

'Right!' *Before he'd made his move. She couldn't want the guy back now...could she?* 'Brendan dumped her, Mum, so don't be getting any romantic ideas about their getting together again,' he said tersely.

'But it might have been only a case of him getting cold feet over commitment, Cole. If he comes face to face with Liz over there...'

'I am not paying for my personal assistant to run off with a guy in Kathmandu!' Cole thundered into the receiver. 'If you assist this in any way whatsoever...'

'Oh, dear! I didn't think of that. Well, I don't think she would actually run off, Cole. As you said, Liz is very responsible. I'm sure she'd insist on Brendan following her back home to prove good faith.'

'Better that the situation be avoided altogether,' he grated through a clenched jaw.

'You can't block Fate, dear,' his mother said blithely.

Fate was a fickle fool, Cole thought viciously, recalling how quickly Liz had agreed to the trip. He'd listed off Nepal as one of the destinations when he put the proposition to her. She must have instantly thought…Kathmandu…Brendan. And she'd played his mother brilliantly at lunch that day, clinching the deal.

No reluctance at the possibility of meeting him over there.

She'd even told his mother where the guy was.

'Mum, you keep your nose right out of this,' Cole commanded. 'No aiding and abetting. I'm telling you straight. Brendan was no good for Liz.'

'No good?' came the critical reply. 'Then why did she stay with him so long? She didn't have a child to consider…like you did with Tara. And Liz didn't do the leaving,' his mother reminded him with pertinent emphasis.

He wanted to shout, *Liz is with me, now,* but knew it would be tantamount to ringing wedding bells in his mother's ears and Cole was not prepared to deal with that.

'He repressed her. He put her down. He made her feel like a failure,' he punched out. 'I know this, Mum, so just let it be. Liz is better off without him. Okay?'

A long pause, then…'You really do care about her, don't you?'

Care? Of course, he cared. And he certainly didn't want to lose her to an idiot who hadn't cared enough to keep her. However, what he needed here was to seal his mother's sympathy to the cause of holding Liz away from Brendan.

'She's had a rough time, Mum,' he said in a gentler tone. 'I want you to ensure she enjoys this trip. No pain.'

'I'll do my best,' came the warm and ready promise.

Mother hen to the rescue of wounded bird.

Cole breathed more easily.

'Right! Well, I hope you have a wonderful time together.'

'Thank you. I'm sure we will. Oh, there's the limousine now. Must go, dear. Goodbye! Thanks for all your help.'

Gone!

He put the receiver down and stared at the telephone for several seconds, strongly tempted to call Liz, but what more could he say? He'd told her last night he would miss her, shown her how very desirable she was to him. There could be no possible doubt in her mind that he wanted her back, wanted her with him.

Surely to God she wouldn't throw what they'd shared aside and take Brendan back!

She couldn't be that much of a fool!

Or did he have it all wrong?

Cole rose from his chair and paced around the office, unsettled by the sudden realisation that much of what he'd told his mother comprised assumptions on his part. Maybe Liz had felt secure enough in her relationship with Brendan not to bother about feminine frippery, saving money towards a marriage and having a family…which had slipped away from her because… *He didn't like my style of management.*

That was all she had actually told him about the relationship.

He'd interpreted the rest.

What if he was wrong?

He'd steamrolled Liz into a hot and heavy affair, to which she'd been a willing party, but he didn't really know what was going on in her mind. Was it rebound stuff for her? An overwhelming need to *feel* desired?

What if she did meet Brendan in Kathmandu and they clicked again, as they must have done in the beginning? Would she count the sex with her boss as meaning anything in any long-term sense? Had he made it *mean* anything to her?

All he'd said was it felt right.

And it did.

She'd agreed.

But was it enough to hold her to him?

Cole didn't know.

But there was nothing more he could do or say now to shift the scales his way.

Besides, Kathmandu was a big city. The tour schedule was jam-packed. The likelihood of her running into Brendan was very low. She had a full-time job to do—looking after his mother—and he'd just ensured, as best he could, that his mother wouldn't let Liz skip out on her responsibility.

Cole took a deep breath and returned to his desk.

Liz would come back.

He was wasting time, worrying over things he had no control over, but that very lack of absolute control where Liz Hart was concerned made him…uneasy.

CHAPTER FOURTEEN

LIZ quickly found she had no difficulty in travelling with Nancy Pierson. All the older woman needed was a bit of prompting on where they had to be at what time, and when their luggage was to be put outside their hotel room to be collected by the Captain's Choice staff, all of whom were brilliantly and cheerfully efficient. Nancy accepted the prompting good-naturedly, grateful that Liz took the responsibility of ensuring they did everything right.

It was quite marvellous flying off on a chartered Qantas jet with almost two hundred other tourists, everyone excited about the adventure ahead of them. The party atmosphere on the plane was infectious, helped along by the champagne which flowed from the moment they were seated.

'Oh, I'm so glad you were able to come with me,' Nancy enthused, her eyes twinkling with the anticipation of much pleasure as she started on a second glass of champagne.

'So am I. This is great. But you want to go easy on the champers, Nancy. Don't drink it too quickly,' Liz warned, concerned about her getting tipsy.

Nancy laughed. 'I'm not a lush, dear. Just celebrating.' She leaned over confidentially. 'Cole's divorce was settled on Thursday. He's completely free of that woman now.'

'Well, I guess that's a good thing,' Liz said non-committally, unsure how she should respond.

'He'd make a wonderful husband to the right woman, you know,' Nancy went on, eyeing her with a spark of hopeful eagerness.

Liz could feel a tide of heat creeping up her neck and quickly brushed the subject aside. 'A failed marriage often puts people off the idea of marrying again.'

'But Cole absolutely adored his son. It was such a terrible tragedy losing David, and it's taken a long time for him to get over it, but I'm sure he'll want to have more children and he's not getting any younger,' Nancy argued.

'Men can have children any time they like,' Liz dryly pointed out. 'It's only women who have a biological clock ticking.'

'He doesn't want to get too old and set in his ways.' A sad sigh. 'His father—my husband—was like that, unfortunately. Didn't want more than one child. But I'm sure Cole is different. He loved being a father.'

'Then perhaps he'll be one again someday.'

This drew a sharp look. 'Do you want children, Liz?'

The flush swept into her cheeks. 'Someday.'

Another sigh. 'Someday I'd love to have a grand-child in my life again. Your mother must be delighted with hers.'

'Yes, she is. Particularly the twins, being boys, after having only daughters herself.'

Luckily, this turn of the conversation diverted

Nancy from pushing Cole as an eligible husband—a highly sensitive issue—and Liz was able to relax again. She didn't want to speculate on her new relationship with Nancy's son. It had happened so fast. She was banking on time away to bring some sort of perspective to it…on both sides.

When they arrived in Kuching, it was great to immerse herself in a completely different part of the world. Their hotel overlooked the Sarawak River with its fascinating traffic of fishing boats and sampans—smells and sights of the East. Kuching actually meant the city of cats and it even had a cat museum featuring an amazing collection of historical memorabilia on the feline species.

On their second morning, a bus took them to the Semengoh Orangutan Reserve where they were able to observe the animals closest to humans on the primate ladder, extinct now except here in Borneo. The orangutans' agility, swinging through the trees, was amazing but it was their eyes that Liz would always remember—so like people's eyes in their expression.

They also visited a long house where over a thousand men, women and children lived together in the old traditional way, with each family having their own quarters but sharing a large verandah as a communal area. No isolation here, as there was in modern apartment buildings, Liz thought. Ready company seemed to make for happy harmony, and sharing was obviously a way of life, clearly giving a sense of security and contentment in continuity.

It made her wonder how much had been lost in striving for singular achievement in western society.

She didn't want to live alone for the rest of her life, yet going back to her parents' home didn't seem right, either. She was thirty years old, had a mortgage on an apartment she was living in, but no one to share it with on any permanent basis. Her neighbours in the apartment block were like ships passing in the night. Where was she going with her life?

Would Cole ever think of marrying her?

Having a family with her?

Or was all this sexual intensity nothing more than a floodgate opening after a long period of celibacy?

It hurt to think about it. She knew the attraction had always been there on her side—suppressed because it had to be. Her boss was off limits for a variety of good reasons. Besides which, he'd shown no interest in her as a woman until…what exactly had triggered his interest? The new image? The fact that Brendan was no longer an item in her life, making her unattached and available? Simple proximity when he felt tempted by Tara's blatantly offered sexuality?

To Liz's mind, it wasn't something solid, something she could trust in any long-term sense. As much as she would like to explore a serious relationship with Cole, she wasn't sure it was going to develop that way, which made her feel very vulnerable about the eventual outcome.

She could end up in a far worse situation than when Brendan had decided enough was enough. Holding on to her job would be unthinkable, unbearable. Did Cole realise that? Had he even paused to think about it? What did *right* mean to him?

She wasn't at all sure that Diana's advice about

going with the flow was good—not if it led to a waterfall that would dash her to pieces. But there was no need to make any decision about it yet. Indeed, she didn't know enough to make a sensible decision.

The next day the tour group had a wonderful boat trip on the river to Bako National Park where they walked through a rainforest and swam in the South China Sea from a beautiful little beach. It felt like a million miles away from the more sophisticated life in Australia—primitive, sensual on a very basic level, simple but very real pleasures. Time slipped by without any worries.

They left Kuching and flew to Rangoon in Burma—or rather Yangon in Myanmar as it was now known. This had been one of the richest countries of South-East Asia and its past glories were abundantly evident. The Shwedagon Pagoda with its giant dome covered with sixty tonnes of gold and the top of the stupa encrusted with thousands of diamonds, rubies and sapphires, was absolutely awesome.

And the comfort of a past era was amply displayed in the old steam train chartered to take the tourists into the nearby countryside, through the green rice fields and the small villages where nothing had changed for centuries. Pot plants decorated the carriages, legroom was spacious, seats were far more comfortable than in modern trains, and provided with drink holders and ashtrays. The windows, of course, could be opened and it was fun waving to the people they passed, all of whom waved back.

'I feel like the queen of England,' Nancy commented laughingly. 'Such fun!'

Indeed, much of England lingered here, especially in the architecture of the city. The City Hall, Supreme and High Court Buildings, GPO, Colonial Offices— all of them would have looked at home in London, yet the city centre revolved around the Sule Pagoda which was stunningly from a very different culture, as were the temples.

On their last night in Rangoon a 'grand colonial evening' had been arranged for them at The Strand Hotel which had been built by an English entrepreneur and opened in 1901. It had once been considered 'the finest hostelry east of Suez, patronised by royalty, nobility and distinguished personages'—according to the 1911 edition of Murray's Handbook for Travelers in India, Burma and Ceylon.

The men were given a pith helmet to put them in the correct British India period, the women an eastern umbrella made of wood and paper printed with flowers. Everyone was asked to wear white as far as possible and as Liz dressed for the evening in the broderie anglaise peasant blouse and frilled skirt that Cole had bought for her, memories of their shopping spree came flooding back.

You're a class act, Liz Hart. Top of the top. And you are going to be dressed accordingly.

Cole hadn't been talking sex then.

If she really was the *top of the top* to him…but maybe that just referred to her efficiency as his P.A.

As much as she wanted to believe he could fall in love with her—was in love with her—Liz felt he only wanted sex, no emotional ties. And she'd been tempted into tasting the realisation of a fantasy which probably should have remained a fantasy. Except she couldn't regret the experience of having actually known what it was like to be his woman, if only for a little while.

'I just love that outfit on you!' Nancy remarked, eyeing her admiringly as they set off from their hotel room.

Liz bit her lips to stop the words, 'Your son's choice.' She forced a smile. 'Well I must say you look spectacular in yours, Nancy.'

She did. Her glittery white tunic was beaded with pearls at the neckline and hem, falling gracefully over a narrow skirt which was very elegant. In fact, Nancy had been right about the dressing on this tour. Casual clothes ruled during the day, but there was very classy dressing at the evening dinners which were invariably a special event.

The compliment was received with obvious pleasure. 'Thank you, dear. We must make the most of this last night here. It's off to Kathmandu tomorrow.'

Liz didn't reply. Kathmandu conjured up thoughts of Brendan. Was he happy with *the space* he'd put between them? If by some weird coincidence they should meet, would he think she had pursued him? What would his reaction be?

Didn't matter, Liz decided with a touch of bitterness. She'd wasted three years on him and wasn't going to waste another minute even thinking about their past relationship. But was she doing any better for herself with Cole? Would she look back in a few months' time and wonder at her own madness for getting so intimately involved with him?

A bus transported them to the Strand Hotel, the men laughing in their helmet hats—a pukka reminder of the British Raj—the women twirling their umbrellas with very feminine pizazz, embracing the sense of slipping back into a past era. They walked into a spacious, very old-world reception lobby, two storeys high with marvellous ceiling fans and chandeliers, wonderful arrangements of flowers, someone playing eastern music on a xylophone. Many waiters circulated with trays of cocktails and hors d'oeuvres, the refreshments adding to the convivial mood.

Overlooking the lobby was an upstairs balcony, a richly polished wood balustrade running around the four sides. Nancy was taking it all in, revelling in the ambience of the superbly kept period hotel. Liz heard her gasp, and automatically looked to where she was looking, her whole body jolting in shock as she saw what Nancy saw.

'Good heavens! There's Cole!'

He was on the balcony scanning the crowd below. Even as his mother spoke, his gaze zeroed in on them. His mouth twitched into a smile. He raised his hand in a brief salute then turned away, heading for the staircase which would bring him down to where they were.

Every nerve in Liz's body was suddenly wired with hyper-tension. Her mind pulsed with wild speculation over why Cole was here? He hadn't once suggested he might catch up with them on this trip. Had he felt compelled to check on her for some reason? Didn't he trust her with his mother?

'Well, well, well,' Nancy drawled, her voice rich

with satisfaction. 'Cole has actually taken time off work to be with us. Isn't that wonderful!'

It jerked Liz out of her turbulent thoughts. 'Did you…invite him to join us?' she choked out, her throat almost too tight to force words out.

Nancy shook her head in a bemused fashion. 'I didn't even think of it.' A lively interest sparkled in her eyes. 'Though I do find it very encouraging that he's done so just before we leave for Kathmandu.'

'Encouraging?' Liz echoed, not comprehending Nancy's point.

'Oh yes, dear. It's a very good sign,' she said with a complacent smile.

Of what?

Liz didn't have time to ask. Cole was already downstairs and heading towards them. He cut such an imposing figure and emanated such powerful purpose, people automatically moved aside to give him a clear path through the milling crowd, heads turning to stare after him, women eyeing him up and down. He looked absolutely stunning dressed in a white linen suit, made classy casual by the black T-shirt he'd teamed it with. A man in a million, Liz thought, her heart pounding erratically at his fast approach.

He grinned, his hands lifting into a gesture that encompassed them both as he reached them. 'Definitely the two best looking women here!' he declared.

His mother laughed. 'What a surprise to see you!'

'A happy one, I hope.' His gaze slid to Liz, the piercing blue eyes suddenly like laser beams burning into hers. The grin softened to a quirky smile. 'One day in the office with your replacement was enough to spur me into taking a vacation. You are…quite irreplaceable, Liz.'

In the office or in his bed? Did this mean he'd decided he couldn't do without her? Excitement fevered her brain. 'Have you arranged to join the tour?'

'Only for this evening. I'm actually booked into this hotel for a couple of days. I thought I'd have this one night with you…'

One night…in this hotel…

'…share what appears to be a very special occasion and escort you both to dinner.' He turned back to his mother. 'Are you enjoying yourself, Mum?'

'Immensely, dear. What are your plans for the rest of your vacation?'

'I thought I'd take a look at Mandalay while I'm in this country. It's always had a fascinating ring to it…Mandalay…'

'You're not coming to Kathmandu?'

'No.' He flicked a quick probing look at Liz. Trying to assess her reaction to this decision? Was she okay with only one night here? 'But I am flying on to Vietnam,' he added. 'I might meet up with you there.'

'We're very busy in Vietnam,' his mother warned.

He laughed. 'Perhaps I'll catch up with you for another dinner together. Hear all your news.'

Another night.

Liz's heart squeezed tight.

Was Cole expecting to whisk her away from his mother for a while…fit in a hot bit of sex?

If so, she wouldn't be a party to it, Liz fiercely decided, her backbone stiffening. She would not have his mother thinking there was some hanky-panky going on between her son and his personal assistant, just as his ex-wife had suggested. Nancy might even leap to a rosy conclusion that was not currently on the cards—marriage and grandchildren!—and her happy allusions to it would be horribly embarrassing.

Best that she didn't so much as guess at any intimate connection. There were another eleven days of the trip to get through and every hour of it in Nancy's company. As it was, she was happily raving on to Cole about what they'd seen so far, accepting his presence here at face value. *Let it stay that way,* Liz grimly willed.

'What about you, Liz? Having fun?' he inquired charmingly.

'Yes, thank you.'

'No problems?' His eyes scoured hers, trying to penetrate the guard she'd just raised.

'None,' she answered sharply.

He frowned slightly. 'I haven't come to check up on you, if that's what you're wondering.'

She managed an ironic smile. 'That would comprise bad judgment and a waste of time and money, Cole.'

He returned her smile. 'As always, your logic is spot on.'

'Thank you. I hope you enjoy your vacation.'

The distance she was putting between them was so obvious in her impersonal replies, he couldn't possibly mistake it. His eyes glittered at her, as though she'd thrown out a challenge he was bent on taking up with every bit of ammunition at his disposal. Liz burned with aggressive determination. Not in front of your mother, she wanted to scream at him.

'Time to move on to the ballroom,' Nancy announced, observing the people around moving forward, being ushered towards the next stage of the evening—dinner, entertainment and dancing in the Strand Hotel ballroom.

'Ladies...'

With mock colonial gallantry, Cole held out both of his arms for them to hook on to, ready to parade them in to dinner. His mother happily complied. Realising it would be rude to try avoiding the close contact, Liz followed suit, fixing a smile on her face and focusing on the people moving ahead of them, doing her level best to ignore the heat emanating from him and jangling every nerve in her body.

As they walked along, Nancy hailed various new acquaintances amongst the tour group, introducing her son, distracting Cole from any concentration on Liz, for which she was intensely grateful. It left her free to glance around the ballroom which was very elegant, panelled walls painted in different shades of pinky beige, huge chandeliers hanging from very high ceilings, a highly polished wooden floor, tables set for ten with white starched tablecloths and all the chairs had skirted white slip covers, adding to the air of pristine luxury.

Nancy insisted they sit at a table on the edge of the circle left free for dancing, saying she wanted to be close to whatever entertainment had been arranged for them. Cole obliged her by steering them to seats which had a direct view of the stage. Other people quickly joined them, making up the table of ten.

Liz was glad of the numbers. Although Cole had seated himself between her and Nancy, at least she had people to talk to on her other side, a good excuse to break any private tete-a-tete he might have in mind.

Even so, he shattered her hastily thought out defences by leaning close and murmuring, 'I look forward to dancing with you tonight.'

Dancing!

Being held in his arms, pressed into whatever contact he manoeuvred, moved right out of his mother's hearing for whatever he wanted to say to her...

Panic churned through Liz's stomach.

How was she going to handle this?

How?

CHAPTER FIFTEEN

Liz barely heard the choir of street children who had been rescued by the World Vision organization. They sang a number of songs. Another troup of children performed a dance. People made speeches she didn't hear at all. Food was placed in front of her and she ate automatically, not really tasting any of it. The man sitting beside her dominated her mind and played havoc with every nerve in her body.

A band of musicians took over the stage. They played a style of old time jazz that was perfect for ballroom dancing. A few couples rose from their tables, happily intent on moving to the music. Any moment now...

She could politely decline Cole's invitation to dance with him. He couldn't force her to accept. But given the level of intimacy there had been between them, he had every right to expect her compliance. A rejection would create an awkwardness that Nancy would inevitably rush into, urging Liz to *enjoy herself*.

She could say her feet were killing her.

Except she hadn't once complained about sore feet on this tour and Nancy might make a fuss about that, too.

Cole set his serviette on the table, pushed back his chair and rose to his feet. The band was playing

'Moon River', a jazz waltz which could only be executed well with very close body contact. Liz's stomach lurched as Cole turned to her, offering his hand.

'Dance, Liz?'

She stared at the hand, riven by a warring tumult of needs.

'Go on, dear,' Nancy urged. 'I'm perfectly happy watching the two of you waltz around.'

There really was no choice. Cole's other hand was already on the back of her chair ready to move it out of her way. Liz stood on jelly-like legs, fiercely resolving not to spend the night with him, no matter how deep the desire he stirred. It was an issue of... of...

She forgot what the issue was as his fingers closed around hers in a firm possessive clasp. An electric charge ran up her arm and short-circuited her brain. It seemed no time at all before his arm had scooped her against the powerful length of his body and his thighs were pushing hers into the seductive glide of the slow waltz.

He lowered his head and murmured in her ear. 'Why aren't I welcome, Liz?'

Her lobe tingled with the warmth of his breath. It was difficult to gather her scattered wits under the physical onslaught of his strong sexuality. The very direct question felt like an attack too, forcing her to explain her guarded behaviour with him.

'I'm with your mother,' she shot out, hoping he would see the need for some sense of discretion.

'So?' he queried, totally unruffled by any embarrassment she might feel about being pressed into some obvious closeness with him.

'It's not right to…' She struggled with the sensitivity of the situation, finally blurting out, '…to give her ideas…about us.'

'What's not right about it?' he countered. 'We're both free to pursue what we want.' His hand slid down the curve of her spine, splaying across the pit of her back, pressing firmly as his legs tangled with hers in an intricate set of steps and turns. 'I want you,' he said, again breathing into her ear. 'I thought you wanted me.'

She jerked her head back, her gaze wildly defying the simmering desire in his eyes. 'That's been private between us.'

'True. But I have no problem with making our private relationship public. And I can't imagine my mother would have any objection to it, either. She likes you.'

Resentment at his lack of understanding flared. 'That's not the point.'

He raised an eyebrow, mocking her contentious attitude. 'What is the point?'

Liz sucked in a quick breath and laid out what he apparently preferred to ignore. 'Nancy will want to think it's serious. She's already expressed her hope to me that you'll marry again and…and provide her with grandchildren.'

'And you don't see marriage on the cards for us?'

It sounded like a challenge to her. As though she had made a decision without telling him. And his eyes were now burning into hers with the determined purpose of finding out precisely what was on her mind.

Liz was flooded with confusion. 'You said…you said you had no intention of marrying again in a hurry.'

'Marry in haste, repent at leisure,' he quoted sardonically. 'Not a mistake I care to repeat. But I can assure you it won't take me three years to make up my mind.'

'Three…years?'

'That's what you spent on Brendan, Liz.'

She shook her head, amazed that he was linking himself in any way to her experience with Brendan. It was all so completely different. Why even compare a blitzkrieg affair to a long siege for commitment? In any event, it reminded her of a failure she preferred to forget. Surely Cole should realise that.

The music stopped.

The dancing stopped.

Cole still held her close, not making any move to disengage or take her back to the table. She dropped her hand from his shoulder, preparing to push out of his embrace. All the other couples were leaving the dance floor.

'Why didn't you tell me Brendan was in Nepal?'

'What?' Startled, her gaze flew up to meet his and was caught in the blaze of fierce purpose glittering at her.

'You heard me,' he stated grimly.

Her mind was whirling over knowledge he couldn't have…unless… 'Did Brendan try to contact me at the office?'

'Is that what you want to hear? Did you contact him with the news you were coming?'

'No...I...' She didn't understand what this was all about.

'Have you left a message for him to meet you in Kathmandu?' Cole bored in.

'It's over!' she cried, trying to cut through to the heart of the situation.

'Not for me, it isn't!' came the harsh retort.

She glanced wildly around the emptied dance floor. 'You're making a spectacle of us, standing here.'

'Then let's take the show on the road. You want private? We'll have private.'

Before Liz could begin to protest, he had her waist firmly grasped and was leading her straight to Nancy who was keenly watching them.

'I don't want private,' Liz muttered fiercely.

'I'm not going to let you take up ignoring me again, nor pretending there's been nothing deeply personal between us. Public or private, Liz. You choose.'

Aggression was pouring from him. He'd blow discretion sky-high if she insisted on staying at the table with the tour group. Liz frantically sought a way out of the dilemma Cole was forcing. Nancy was smiling at them, pleased to see them linked together. Liz inwardly recoiled from the interpretation she would put on their *togetherness* if Cole made it clear he was involved with his P.A. on more than a professional level.

Best to seize the initiative before he said something. Liz managed a rueful smile as they closed on his mother and quickly spoke up. 'Nancy, Cole and I have some business to sort out. Will you excuse us for a few minutes?'

'Might take quite a while,' Cole instantly inserted. 'Are you okay to get back to your hotel with the tour group, Mum?'

'Of course, dear.' She beamed triumphantly. 'I even have my room key with me. Liz always checks me on that.'

Trapped by her own efficiency.

'I'm sure we won't be so long, Cole,' she said, trying to minimise this *private* meeting.

'Best to cover all eventualities,' he smoothly returned. 'Given we run late sorting out this business, Mum, I'll escort Liz to your hotel and see her safely to your room, so no need to stay up and worry about her.'

Heat whooshed up Liz's neck and scorched her cheeks. Cole had to be planning more than just talk…

'Fine, dear,' came the ready acceptance to her son's plan. Nancy smiled benevolently at Liz. 'And don't you worry about disturbing me. It's been such a very busy day I'm sure I'll sleep like a log.'

Another excuse wiped out.

Cole picked up Liz's small evening bag from the table, taking possession of her money and her room key. 'Thanks, Mum,' he said by way of taking leave, then forcefully shepherded Liz towards the exit from the ballroom.

'Give me my bag,' she seethed through clenched teeth, determined not to have control taken completely out of her hands. If driven to it, she could arrange a taxi for herself.

'Going to do a runner on me, Liz?' he mocked.

'I don't like being boxed into a corner.'

'Right!' He passed it to her. 'So now you're a lady of independent means. Before you trot off in high dudgeon at my interference with your plans, I would appreciate your telling me what use I've been to you, apart from giving you a free ticket to Kathmandu.'

'What *use?*' She halted, stunned by what felt like totally unfair accusations. 'I didn't ask you for a free ticket!'

'This is not a private place.' To prove his point, he waved at the groups of smokers who had gathered out in the foyer to the ballroom. 'Since you don't want to cause gossip that might reach my mother's ears...'

He scooped her along with him, down the steps and through the passage to the hotel lobby, moving so fast Liz had barely caught her breath when he pressed the wall button beside an elevator.

'I am not going to your room,' she declared, furious at his arrogant presumption that she would just fall in with what he wanted.

His eyes seared hers in a savage assault. 'You had no problem with doing so last week.'

Liz's heart galloped at the sheer ferocity of feeling emanating from him. 'That...that was different.'

'How was it different? I'm making this as private as you had it then. Or was I just a stepping stone to boost your confidence enough to win with Brendan tomorrow?'

Brendan again!

The elevator doors opened while Liz was still shell-shocked by Cole's incredible reading of her actions.

He bundled her into the compartment and they were on their way up before her mind could even begin to encompass what he was implying. She stared at him in dazed disbelief. 'You think I went to bed with you to boost my confidence?'

'A frequent rebound effect,' he shot at her.

She was so incensed by the realisation he actually did think she had *used* him, the reverse side of that coin flooded into her mind. 'What about you, Cole?' she shot back at him. 'Quite a coincidence that on the very day Tara suggested I was obliging you in bed, you decided to make that true.'

He looked appalled. 'Tara had nothing to do with what I felt that night. Absolutely nothing!'

'So why do you imagine Brendan had anything to do with what I felt?'

'You didn't want the light on.'

'I didn't want you comparing me to your hot-shot wife. Finding me much less sexy.'

'You think I'd even look at a Tara clone after what I've been through with her?' he thundered.

Liz was stung into retorting, 'I don't know. She was the woman you married.'

'And divorced. As soon as it could be decently achieved after the death of our child.' A hard pride settled on his face. 'Tara is a user. She doesn't give a damn for anyone but herself. And believe me, that becomes sickeningly *unsexy* after you've lived with it for a while.' His eyes flashed venomously at her as he added, 'And I don't take kindly to being used by a woman I thought better of.'

'I didn't use you,' Liz cried vehemently.

'No? Then why the freeze-off tonight?'

'I told you. Your mother…'

'Not good enough!' he snapped, just as the elevator doors opened. He hustled her out into a corridor, jammed a key in a door, and pulled her into a private suite that ensured they'd be absolutely alone together.

Liz didn't fight the flow of action. The realisation had finally struck that this was not about having sex with her tonight. It was about sorting out their relationship and what it meant to them. And Cole was in a towering rage because he believed she meant to meet Brendan tomorrow, with the possible purpose of reigniting interest in a future together.

He released his hold on her as he closed the door behind them, apparently satisfied he had shut off all avenues of escape. 'Now…now I'll have the truth from you,' he said, exuding a ruthless relentlessness that perversely sent a thrill through Liz.

He cared.

He really cared.

Hugging this sweet knowledge to herself she walked on into the massive suite, past the opened door to a huge bathroom, past two queen size beds, through an archway to an elegant sitting room. She turned to face him in front of the large curtained window at the far end. He'd followed her to the archway where he stood with an air of fierce patience—a big, powerful man who was barely reining in violent feelings.

'I didn't tell you Brendan was in Nepal because it was irrelevant to us, Cole,' she stated quietly.

'Hardly irrelevant,' he gravelled back at her. 'Because of him you stopped hiding your light under a bushel and showed me a Liz Hart I'd never seen before.'

She shook her head. 'That was my sisters' idea. To brighten me up so that other men might see me as attractive. My mother insisted it would make me feel better about myself. Brendan was gone, Cole. I never thought for one moment of trying to get him back. It was over.'

'But then…having made me see you differently, which led to my proving how very desirable you were…you had a ticket to Nepal in your hand—the chance to show Brendan what he was missing.'

'We're going to Kathmandu. I have no idea where in Nepal Brendan is or if, indeed, he's still there. I don't care. If by some freakish chance I should run into him, it won't make any difference. I don't ever want him in my life again.'

He frowned. 'Is that how you feel about me, too? I've served your purpose of…feeling better about yourself?'

She lifted her chin in a kind of defiant challenge, telling herself she had nothing to lose now. 'You want the truth, Cole?'

'Yes.' Piercing blue eyes demanded it of her.

'I've always been attracted to you. But you were married. And I was no Tara Summerville anyway so it was absurd of me to even dream of ever having you. I guess you could say Brendan was a pragmatic choice for me and I tried quite desperately to make it work. Maybe that was what drove him away in the end…me trying too hard to make something that was never quite right into something I could live with.'

Another frown. 'You never indicated an attraction…'

'That would have been futile. And I liked working with you.'

He grimaced and muttered, 'My oasis in a desert.'

'Pardon?'

He managed an ironic smile. 'You helped make my life livable during its darkest days, just by being there, Liz.'

Her smile was wry. 'The handmaiden.'

'Oh, I wouldn't put you in that category. A handmaiden wouldn't talk back, put me in my place. More a helpmate.'

Liz took a deep breath and spilled out the critical question for her. 'Was I helping you to shut Tara out of your mind in those days—and nights—before your divorce was settled?'

He shook his head, clearly vexed by such a concept. 'She was gone. A lot longer gone than Brendan was for you, Liz. Part of me was angry because he'd made you feel a failure, made you feel less than you are. And Tara had put you down, as well. I wanted to lift you up…

'You took…*pity*…on me?' Everything within her recoiled from that idea.

'Good God, no!' He looked totally exasperated, frustrated by her interpretation, scowling as he gathered his thoughts to dispel it. 'I was angry that you felt so low, especially since you were worth so much more than the people who did that to you. I tried to tell you…show you….' He lifted his hands in an oddly helpless gesture. 'In the end, I couldn't stop myself from making love to you even though I knew I shouldn't risk our business relationship.'

'Making love…' She struggled to swallow the huge lump that had risen in her throat. 'It did feel like that, but then it seemed you only had sex on your mind. All the sex you could get.'

'With you, Liz. Only with you.' His eyes softened, warmed, simmered over her. 'You truly were like an oasis in the desert and when I finally got there, I wanted to revel in everything you gave me. It felt so good.'

So good… She couldn't deny it, didn't want to shade that truth by other things, but she needed to have all her doubts cleared away.

'To me, too,' she admitted. 'But I thought…maybe I was just handy and you were using me to…'

'No. Simply because you're you, Liz.'

'Tonight…when I saw you here…I decided I didn't want to be used like that. Not even by you, Cole.' She held tightly on to all her courage as she added, 'Though I want you more than any man I've known.'

His face broke into a smile that mixed relief with intense pleasure. 'Believe me. The feeling is entirely mutual.'

She let out the breath that had been caught in her lungs and an answering smile burst across her face. 'Really?'

'What do you think I've been fighting for?' He swiftly crossed the short distance between them and wrapped her in a tight hug, his eyes burning into hers with very serious intent. 'No pulling away from me now. We're going to see how well this relationship can work for us. Give it time. Okay?'

Not an impossible dream.

It was almost too much to believe. Her heart swelled with glorious hope. Her mind danced with future possibilities. She was being held very possessively by the man she wanted more than any other in the world. He'd left his work and flown to South-East Asia to fight anything that might part them, and now he was saying...

'Answer me, Liz.'

Commanding...

She loved this man...everything about him. Her arms flew up around his neck. 'Yes, Cole. Yes.' Joy in her voice, desire churning through her body. Mutual, she thought exultantly.

He kissed her, making *mutual* absolutely awesome.

They made love...wonderful, passionate, blissful love...long into the night. No inhibitions. Cole didn't have to sweep them away. Liz felt none. She believed she was the woman he wanted in every sense. He made her feel it. There was nothing she couldn't do with him, nothing she couldn't say to him. And she no longer worried about what his mother might think. Nancy would be happy for them.

It was almost dawn when Cole arranged for a car to transport them to the tour hotel. They'd both decided his mother might panic if Liz wasn't in their room when she woke up. Liz felt too exhilarated to sleep at all. She told herself she would have the opportunity later this morning, on the flight to Kathmandu.

Which reminded her…

'How did you know Brendan was in Nepal, Cole?'

'My mother told me, just before leaving on the trip.'

'Your mother?' Liz frowned over this unexpected source until she recollected having answered Nancy's questions on her ex-boyfriend. 'But why would she do that?'

Cole smiled. 'Maybe she guessed I cared about you and the suggestion that I might lose you was a prompt to action if I wanted to keep you.'

Liz sighed with happy contentment. 'Well, I'm glad you came.'

Cole squeezed her hand. 'So am I.'

She glanced down at their interlocked hands, suddenly recalling the horribly tense scene just after Tara had left the Palm Beach house and Cole had come to the conservatory to eliminate any distress she'd caused.

'Well, isn't that nice?' his mother had remarked. 'He cares about you, dear.'

Liz could now smile over the memory.

Maybe mothers knew best.

Cole did care about her.

And Liz certainly felt very, very good about herself.

CHAPTER SIXTEEN

Six months later…

LIZ and her sisters were in the kitchen, cleaning up after the Sunday lunch barbecue—an informal family celebration of her engagement to Cole who was happily chatting to her father and brothers-in-law out on the patio. Her mother and Nancy Pierson had their heads together in the lounge room, conferring about the wedding which Cole had insisted be held as soon as it could be arranged.

'That man of yours truly is charming. And mouth-wateringly attractive,' Sue declared, rolling her eyes teasingly at Liz. 'You have to admit it now.'

She laughed. 'He's improved a lot since we've been together.'

'Oh, you!' Sue flicked a tea-towel at her. 'You never give anything away. Still all buttoned up within yourself.'

'No, she's not!' Diana instantly disagreed. 'She's positively blossomed since we made her over. Best idea I ever had. And look what's come out of it.' She grabbed Liz's left hand out of the sink of washing up water and suds. 'Got to see your gorgeous ring again!'

It was a magnificent ruby, surrounded by diamonds. Liz smiled at the red gleams as Diana turned it to the light.

'That's the fire in you,' Cole had said when he'd slid it on her finger. 'Every time I think of you I feel warm.' Then a wicked grin. 'If not hot.'

'This is a very serious ring,' Diana decided. 'Definitely a *to have and to hold from this day forth* ring. High-powered stuff. I hope you realise what you're getting into with this guy, Liz.'

'I have known Cole for quite some time,' she answered dryly.

It evoked a gurgle of gleeful amusement. 'Nothing like marrying the boss.'

'What impresses me…' Jayne chimed in. '…is how good he is with the children. He's like a magnet to them. They're all over him and he obviously doesn't mind a bit.'

'He doesn't. Cole loved being a father.'

Jayne heaved a rueful sigh. 'So sad about the son he lost. Is he mad keen to have a family with you, Liz?'

'Definitely keen.'

'Liz…' her mother called from the doorway. 'Would you go and fetch Cole inside to us. Nancy and I need to talk to both of you.'

'Okay, Mum.'

Liz dried her hands on Jayne's tea-towel and headed for the patio. Behind her, her three sisters broke into a raucous chorus of, 'Here comes the bride…'

Liz was laughing at their high-spirited good humour as she stepped outside. It was so good to feel at one with them instead of shut out of their charmed circle, looking in. Not that they had ever shut her out.

Liz realised now she'd done that to herself, not feeling she could ever compete with them.

It was only with Cole that she'd come to understand that love had nothing to do with competition. Love simply accepted who you were. You didn't have to be like someone else...just who you were.

And she saw his love for her in his eyes as she walked towards him. It warmed her all through, made her feel special and brilliantly alive. She smiled, loving him right back.

'Our mothers want us in the lounge room with them. I think you've thrown them a bit, insisting on a quick wedding.'

'No way are we going to put it off,' he warned, and promptly excused himself from the company of the other men. He reached her in a couple of strides and wrapped an arm around her shoulders. 'We're standing firm on this, Liz. I want us married. I'm not waiting a day longer than I have to.'

'They won't be happy if they can't organise a proper wedding. And just remember, I only intend to be a bride once.'

He slanted a look at her that crackled with powerful purpose. 'I promise you, you'll have a proper wedding.'

Cole really was unstoppable when he had a goal in his sights.

Once they were in the lounge room, their mothers regaled them with the plans they'd made. A Saturday would be best for the wedding. Impossible to book a decent reception place at such short notice. Nancy had offered her home at Palm Beach, a marquee to be put up over the grounds surrounding the pool. Catering could be arranged.

'But, Liz,' her mother addressed her seriously. 'We really should have six weeks for the invitations to go out. People need that much time to…'

'No,' Cole broke in decisively. 'A month is it. If some invited guests can't make it, I'm sorry but we're not waiting on them.'

'What is the hurry, dear?' Nancy cried in exasperation.

His piercing blue eyes speared the question at Liz.

She nodded, feeling sure enough now to share their secret.

'Liz wouldn't agree to marry me until she was three months pregnant and feeling secure that everything was okay and she'd carry our baby full term.'

'Pregnant?' Her mother gaped at Liz.

'A baby!' Nancy clapped her hands in delight.

'If I'd had my way, we would have been married before she got pregnant,' Cole informed them. 'But Liz got this fixation about having a child…'

'*Our* child,' Liz gently corrected him.

He gave her a look that melted her bones. '*Our* child,' he repeated in a thrilling tone of possessive pride and joy.

'A grandchild,' Nancy said on a sigh of pleasure.

'And Liz doesn't want to look lumpy in her wedding dress,' Cole went on.

'Of course not!' Nancy happily agreed.

'Liz…' Having recovered from her initial shock, her mother rose from her armchair, shaking her head at her daughter as she came over to enfold her in a motherly hug. '…always bent on doing it your way. Congratulations, darling.'

'I'm so happy, Mum,' Liz assured her.

'As you should be.'

'And I'm so happy for both of you,' Nancy declared, leaving her chair to do some hugging herself. 'Liz is the right woman for you, Cole. I knew it the moment I met her.'

'Amazing how anyone can be blessed with such certainty at a moment's notice,' Cole drawled, his eyes twinkling at Liz.

'Mother's intuition,' she archly informed him. 'Maybe I'll get some of that myself in six months' time.'

'Mmmh…removing logical argument from our relationship?'

'More like shortcutting it.'

'This might be stretching my love for you.'

'You swore it would stretch on forever.'

He turned to his mother. 'You see, Mum? She's too smart for me.'

'Go on with you, Cole,' Nancy laughingly chided. 'You love it.'

He grinned. 'Yes, I do. And since we now have the wedding back on track, I'm going to whisk Liz off to show her how very much I love everything about her.'

And he did.

Six months later, Liz and Cole were the besotted parents of a baby daughter, Jessica Anne, whose tiny fingers curled around one of her father's and instantly enslaved him for life.

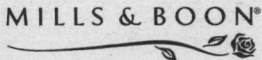

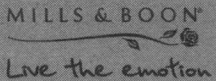

MILLS & BOON®

Live the emotion

Modern Romance™

McGILLIVRAY'S MISTRESS by Anne McAllister

Fiona Dunbar isn't ready for the return of Lachlan McGillivray to Pelican Cay. His roguish reputation goes before him, and soon the whole island is certain they are having an affair! But Fiona wants to live life on her own terms. If Lachlan wants her he'll have to make her his bride!

THE TYCOON'S VIRGIN BRIDE by Sandra Field

Twelve years ago, Jenessa's secret infatuation with tycoon Bryce Laribee turned to passion – but when he discovered she was a virgin he walked out! Now, the attraction between them is just as intense, and Bryce is determined to finish what they started. But Jenessa has a secret or two...

THE ITALIAN'S TOKEN WIFE by Julia James

Furious at his father, Italian millionaire Rafaello di Viscenti vows to marry the first woman he sees – Magda, a single mother desperately trying to make ends meet by doing his cleaning! Rafaello's proposal comes with a financial reward, so Magda has no choice but to accept...

A SPANISH ENGAGEMENT by Kathryn Ross

The future of Carrie Michaels' orphaned niece is threatened and there is only one answer: find a man and pretend she's engaged! Carrie can't believe her luck when sexy Spanish lawyer Max Santos offers to help – but little does she realise that Max has needs of his own...

On sale 6th February 2004

Available at most branches of WHSmith, Tesco, Martins, Borders, Eason, Sainsbury's and all good paperback bookshops.

0104/01b

4 FREE

books and a surprise gift!

We would like to take this opportunity to thank you for reading this Mills & Boon® book by offering you the chance to take FOUR more specially selected titles from the Modern Romance™ series absolutely FREE! We're also making this offer to introduce you to the benefits of the Reader Service™—

- ★ FREE home delivery
- ★ FREE gifts and competitions
- ★ FREE monthly Newsletter
- ★ Exclusive Reader Service offers
- ★ Books available before they're in the shops

Accepting these FREE books and gift places you under no obligation to buy, you may cancel at any time, even after receiving your free shipment. Simply complete your details below and return the entire page to the address below. *You don't even need a stamp!*

YES! Please send me 4 free Modern Romance books and a surprise gift. I understand that unless you hear from me, I will receive 6 superb new titles every month for just £2.60 each, postage and packing free. I am under no obligation to purchase any books and may cancel my subscription at any time. The free books and gift will be mine to keep in any case.

P4ZED

Ms/Mrs/Miss/Mr ....Initials..
BLOCK CAPITALS PLEASE

Surname ....

Address ....

....

....Postcode.................................

Send this whole page to:
UK: FREEPOST CN81, Croydon, CR9 3WZ
EIRE: PO Box 4546, Kilcock, County Kildare (stamp required)